MORTAL GODS

Annabel Claridge

Hemington Publishing

First published in 2008
by Hemington Publishing Limited
18 Magdalens Road, Ripon, HG4 1HX

www.hemingtonpublishing.co.uk

ISBN 978-0-9558142-1-1

Printed in Great Britain
A CIP catalogue record is available for this book from
The British Library

For my own ma, Una Claridge
1928-2002

The following story is based on actual events

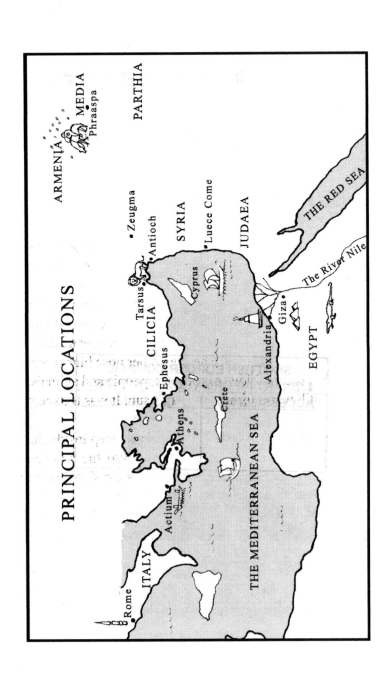

PRINCIPAL LOCATIONS

CHAPTER ONE

Off the coast of Alexandria, Egypt.
October 48BC

The ship's sails had been lowered, her oars withdrawn, her lamps extinguished. Now she was anonymous, almost invisible against the vast waters and the inky sky.

On the vessel's upper deck, towards the prow, a small black poodle stood silhouetted in the moonlight. Her head and tail were raised, and her ears streamed out behind her in the breeze. She tipped her nose higher and caught the scent of flowers and fruit, people and animals, and soil still warm from yesterday's sun. It was the scent of land. Her land. She was almost home.

When she felt a sudden rumble from deep inside the belly of the ship, she dug her claws into the wooden boards to steady herself. She listened for a rush of chains and heard an almighty splash as the anchor shot forward and plummeted to the sea bed. The ship shuddered, and the poodle shook the sea spray from her fur, sighed happily and trotted belowdecks to her private cabin.

She flopped onto her zebra skin blanket, curled up against its warmth and tried to sleep, but it was impossible. The smells of her homeland had flooded her mind with memories and expectations.

A few months earlier, when she'd been barely weaned, she'd been taken from her mother and siblings by someone called Menander. She'd liked Menander immediately. He'd worn long flowing robes and rows of bangles along his arms. He'd carried her out of the house where she'd been born and placed her in a golden basket. She'd never travelled in such a thing before, never travelled in anything, and her tiny stomach had lurched when four men had raised the basket off the ground. She'd let out a cry of desperation then, and Menander had reached out to pat and comfort her.

'I'm here,' he'd told her. 'I will always be here.'

He'd nodded to the men and they'd settled the basket on their shoulders and carried it away from the house, out through its gates, and onto the streets of Alexandria. Hundreds of people had lined the way. They'd been cheering noisily, too noisily for a small puppy's delicate ears. At first she'd trembled and cowered against the basket's sides, but then Menander had patted her again and pointed with his free arm.

'Look at the people,' he'd asked her. 'Let them see you. Bestow your blessings upon them. They cheer for you.'

She'd edged upwards a fraction then, and when she'd realised that just the sight of the top of her head made the crowd leap and roar with approval, she'd found new courage. Soon, she'd been sitting bolt upright and revelling in the attention.

The men had set her down outside a fabulous palace and Menander had lifted her into his arms. For the next few days they'd lived side by side in the palace, a cool, quiet haven with gleaming white colonnades and gardens full of statues, fountains and scented blossom. Menander hadn't left her sight. Even at night he'd been there, lulling her in a haze of incense, singing softly until she fell asleep, and staying with her in case she awoke. During the days, he'd fed her by hand with exquisite foods and taken her for gentle walks in the grounds. Through it all, he'd treated her as if she were the most precious thing in the world.

Then, quite suddenly one morning, he'd shaken her awake when it was still dark outside.

'Our mistress has sent for you,' he'd explained as he packed a bag with treats, toys and blankets. 'One of her bodyguards is waiting outside. He will take you to her.'

He'd picked her up, held her out in front of him and looked at her steadily.

'Be the bearer of good fortune,' he'd whispered. 'Help our mistress to quit her place of exile and return to her throne. All hail you! All await your homecoming and that of our queen!'

She'd had no idea what he was talking about, but she'd licked his hands with her small pink tongue, and he'd laughed and kissed her before carrying her out of the palace and handing her over to the bodyguard.

The bodyguard was a desert tribesman with black eyes

and an even blacker cloak. He'd ridden for two days, enveloping her in his cloak and holding her close to his chest as his horse sped across hot, dusty plains. At last they'd reached a modest town, and the horse had skidded to a halt outside a merchant's house. Within moments, the door to the house had opened and a young woman with olive skin and a wide smile had rushed through it and run to greet them.

'My name is Cleopatra,' the young woman had said excitedly, 'and I am your new mistress. *I* shall be your mother, now. I will call you Doris. Doris Of The Lovely Hair, and we will be the best of friends.'

Cleopatra had lifted Doris from the horse and taken her into the house. Then she'd unpacked Menander's bag of toys and blankets, (the treats had been eaten along the way), and produced a collar and lead.

'I did not know your size,' she'd apologised as she tied the collar around Doris's neck. 'I had my handmaiden, Charmion, make it for you. The cloth is woven from the hair of a baby camel. It is very fine and will be soft on your skin, but it may be too loose.'

She'd stepped back and laughed.

'It is a *little* large!' she'd giggled as the collar dangled at Doris's knees. 'No matter. You will grow into it. Come. Let us walk together! Soon I must meet with my advisors. You shall come too. Your presence may inspire us.'

That meeting with the advisors had been the first of many. Doris had spent them curled up on her mistress's lap, from where she'd listened to much argument and discussion about a queen, how she might be returned to her rightful throne, and what could be done about someone called Ptolemy.

Doris had wondered if this was the same queen and throne that Menander had talked about but, before she could learn the answer, she'd been woken in the middle of the night again. This time, she'd ridden with Cleopatra. They'd left the village under cover of darkness and, led by mysterious guides on stealthy Arab horses, had crossed yet more dusty plains until they'd reached the sea. There, in a hidden cove, a rowing boat had been waiting to take them out to a ship, this ship. The ship that had sailed them here, to somewhere off the coast of Alexandria.

Doris was almost back where she'd started.

Almost home.

'Nearly there,' she mumbled as she wriggled deeper into her zebra skin. 'By this time tomorrow, I should be back on dry land. I hope Menander will be waiting for me. Will the streets be thronging with people as they were before? Will they cheer and bow to me? It doesn't matter if they don't. I have my mistress, now. But I *would* like to see Menander again.'

She had just reached that lovely, dozing-off stage which comes before real sleep when she heard someone tiptoe into her cabin and whisper her name.

'Doris?' a voice asked. 'Are you awake?'

Doris didn't need to open her eyes. She knew that the voice belonged to Cleopatra's handmaiden, Charmion, the same Charmion who'd made the oversized collar.

'My mistress has probably sent for me,' Doris concluded as Charmion picked her up. 'She likes to cuddle me at night. Soon I will be snuggled up beside her. We will fall asleep together and, when the sun comes up, we'll be rowed ashore.'

She laid her head against Charmion's shoulder and felt the handmaiden's arms curl around her and carry her and her blanket out of the room.

Back on the upper deck, Doris sniffed the wonderful scents again. The sea breeze ruffled her fur and fluttered her blanket, and Charmion's bare feet padded over the boards.

Suddenly, though, something was wrong.

Charmion's body had tensed. Her movements had become tentative, and her graceful walk had slowed to a hesitant totter.

Doris woke with a jolt, forced open her eyes and looked down.

Charmion was standing at the top of a flight of steps, steps that plunged steeply and disappeared into the black waters of the Mediterranean Sea.

Doris wriggled, but Charmion tightened her grip with one hand, grabbed hold of the steps' safety rail with the other and continued downwards.

Again, Doris tried to break free.

Again, Charmion tightened her grip.

The waters rose higher. They splashed against the steps and lapped at Charmion's toes.

For the first time in her life, Doris tried to bark. The noise she made was hardly more than a weak yap, but it seemed to alarm Charmion, who let go of the safety rail to tap her on the nose.

'Hush,' she whispered. 'Listen. Do you hear?'

Doris stopped struggling and tipped her head.

Somewhere in the darkness, something was making a soft, swishing sound. She turned and saw a rowing boat pull away from the shadow of the ship's hull. She peered through the gloom and recognised the strong back and shoulders of its oarsman. It was Apollodorus, one of her mistress's friends. He drew the boat closer and it slid into the moonlight.

Seated against its stern was Cleopatra.

Apollodorus reached the foot of the steps and stretched out a hand to pull his boat hard up against them. Doris expected Cleopatra to leave the rowing boat and board the ship, but she didn't move.

'Come to me, Doris,' she said instead. 'Let Apollodorus bring you. Have no fear, my darling. It is quite safe.'

Doris yelped and dug her claws into Charmion's flesh, but she couldn't contest the oarsman's strong hands. She felt them prize away her paws and take her firmly in their grasp. Then they whisked her over the fearsome gap between the ship and the boat and lowered her safely down.

Doris shook herself and blinked.

'Come here, my sweet,' Cleopatra whispered.

Doris tottered unsteadily across the planked bottom

of the boat until she noticed something tucked under one of the seats. She paused briefly to examine it. It was rolled up tightly, like a scroll. Unlike a scroll, though, it was several paces long and smelled of wool and human feet.

It was a carpet.

'How very peculiar,' Doris muttered to herself, 'why would a carpet be in a rowing boat? Come to think of it, why am *I* in a rowing boat? And why does everything have to happen in the middle of the night?'

She continued to the wooden bench at the stern, leapt onto Cleopatra's lap and nestled against her.

'Pull away,' Cleopatra ordered.

Apollodorus rowed in silence. The only sounds to be heard were the swish of the boat's oars and the slapping of the waves against its sides.

Doris looked from right to left. There was a silver path where the moon reflected on the water, but beyond that she could see nothing but impenetrable darkness. She raised her head. The sky was glittering with stars, and a ball of golden flames was hovering high in the distance. She stood up, wagged her tail, and placed her front paws on the gunwale.

'That's the Pharos!' she yapped in her puppyish way. 'That's the lighthouse at Alexandria! I'm nearly home, ma. I'm nearly home!'

'Sshht!'

Cleopatra clamped a hand over Doris's snout and dragged her into a sitting position.

'You must be very quiet now, my love,' she added gently, 'quiet as a mouse.'

They reached the mouth of the harbour, and Apollodorus removed his oars from the water and allowed the tide to carry the boat to a quay. Once there, he tied the boat to a metal ring and silently helped Doris and her mistress up some slippery stone steps and onto dry land.

There they stood, huddled together in the dark, whilst Apollodorus returned to the boat and retrieved the carpet. He heaved it onto the dock, cut the twine that bound it and gave it a shove with his foot so that it unravelled along the ground. Then he bent over and tugged at its corners until everything was flat. Meanwhile, Cleopatra had thrown aside her shawl and gathered her skirts around her knees. Now she lay down on the carpet.

'Come,' she whispered as she patted the space beside her. 'Lie here, with me.'

Doris glanced at Apollodorus.

'She means you, Doris,' he said.

Doris hesitated and took a step backwards, but the oarsman scooped her up and passed her to her mistress.

'Quickly, now,' Cleopatra urged.

More bemused than ever, Doris did as she'd been asked, but no sooner had she lain down than Apollodorus began to roll the carpet up again. He wrapped it tightly, its living contents were pinned together inside it, and Doris squirmed into a more comfortable position. She felt a tug as Apollodorus tied the carpet with new twine, and a dizzying flip as he hoisted the whole lot into the air and settled it onto his shoulder.

Apollodorus carried the carpet and its contents carefully. He paused every so often to hitch everything back into position and adjust his hold, but then suddenly stopped completely.

Cleopatra's hand moved in the dark.

'Sshht,' she tapped Doris's nose, 'don't bark. Whatever you do, don't bark.'

Doris listened through the carpet and heard someone ask Apollodorus what he was doing.

'Delivering a carpet,' Apollodorus replied.

His tone suggested that the questioner was an idiot.

'Idiot,' thought Doris.

Apollodorus walked on, and Doris sniffed.

Beyond the mustiness of the carpet, the outside air was filled with delicious scents. Doris could smell fruit and flowers, hot spice and cool citrus, and something else besides; the distinctive incense from the fabulous white palace. Just then, Apollodorus was stopped and quizzed again. Again he stated the obvious, but this time his questioner called for assistance.

'Guards!' the man yelled.

Doris heard running footsteps, clanking armour and shuffling noises, and several more men surrounded the carpet.

'They will escort you,' the man added, and Doris suddenly realised he wasn't speaking Egyptian or Greek, which were the usual languages of Alexandria, but Latin.

'He's probably just practicing,' she decided. 'To learn a new language, you have to practice.'

Doris knew this because she and her mistress had recently been learning Latin, too. Their teacher had been none other than Apollodorus himself, who had originally come from Italy. Cleopatra had talked a lot about Italy during the journey home. Its people were called Romans and their leader was a man named Julius Caesar. Cleopatra had described him as an all-conquering hero who was worshipped as a god. Doris thought he sounded like the most terrifying man she'd never met.

Apollodorus marched forward between the guards and Doris felt her mistress's heart pound. She heard the front doors to the white palace swing open, heard the hard clack of feet in its marble corridors and the gentle strumming of musicians in its secret alcoves. She could smell the incense more deeply now. It was permeating the carpet and tickling her nose. She wanted to sneeze. Apollodorus reached a new set of doors and Doris's stomach lurched as he walked through them, swivelled the carpet from his shoulder and lowered it onto the floor. Doris felt him kneel and cut its binding again, felt the twine snap against his knife. She felt the carpet relax and spring free as his soft boot nudged her back and sent her and Cleopatra rolling over and over until the carpet was fully unfurled and they had spilled out of it.

Puffs of dust and carpet fluff swirled around them and Doris struggled to her feet and shook herself.

Someone laughed out loud and Doris glanced up.

Before her sat a man.

He was wearing a newly pressed white linen tunic with gold-fringed sleeves. His hair was thinning, and the little he had left had been brushed forward into a wispy fringe, which peeked out from under a wreath of laurel leaves made of beaten gold. His legs and arms were tanned, and he had beady black eyes, high cheekbones and a heavily muscled neck.

He threw back his head and laughed again.

The rich, deep sound echoed against the palace's vast walls, and Doris stared open-mouthed. She held her breath and turned to see her mistress's reaction. When Cleopatra got calmly to her feet, smoothed down her crumpled clothes and smiled, Doris bared her teeth and tried to smile too.

CHAPTER TWO
Later that day

Doris had been hoping to see Menander again, and now she did. When she'd stopped bouncing with joy, he gathered her up and carried her a short distance through the palace.

'We have been very busy whilst you were gone,' he told her. 'Your mistress is most pleased with you. She even sent instructions from abroad that no expense should be spared to make you feel at home on your return. The best craftsmen in Alexandria and the finest fabrics from the east have been employed to furnish your salon.'

He reached an ivory door. A large triangular Greek letter Δ - D for Doris - had been carved into it and picked out with gold leaf. The door's mouldings were gilded, too, and its handle was made from a single, massive amethyst. Menander turned this handle and pushed the door open.

'Look, Doris,' he breathed. 'This is your room.'

It was built from polished limestone, like the rest of the palace, but the hardness of its walls had been softened with fine woollen curtains. In the centre of the floor was a circular dog bed made of two solid silver cobras. Their tails were intertwined to make an entrance to the bed, and their heads reared up on either side to form handles. Inside the bed were a camel hair mattress, several small blankets and a smattering of miniature, silk-covered cushions.

'That is your bed,' said Menander.

With Doris in his arms, he wandered around the room whilst pointing out and explaining some of its special features.

'Here are water dishes, and these are various food bowls. Here, some incense burners, candles, and vessels for your tit-bits.'

He reached a little dressing table. It had a swivel mirror and was laid with a golden tray covered in an assortment of carefully aligned brushes, combs and hairpins. Doris noticed that some of these had been decorated with sea creatures. There was a silver-backed brush etched with dolphins, and two combs in the shape of sea-horses.

'Doris was a sea goddess,' Menander explained. 'She is sometimes called Doris Of The Lovely Hair. So your name is well chosen, since you have lovely hair, too. I shall enjoy taking care of it as your mistress commands.'

He turned away from the tray and placed Doris in her bed.

'Your bathing room is next door. It has underfloor heating, of course, and a sunken bath. You'll see it later, but now it is time for your nap. You have water and food but don't hesitate to bark, should you need me. I will be just outside. When you awake, we will go for a walk in the gardens.'

He bent to kiss her head.

'Sleep well, sweet Doris,' he said. 'Welcome home.'

When Menander had gone, Doris turned circles on the bed until she'd pummelled a nest, then lay down and curled herself into a ball. As she began to doze off, her thoughts turned to her mistress and the man who'd laughed at her. She had no idea who he was. She didn't even know who her mistress was. Yet it was as though Cleopatra had known all along that the man would be there, as though she'd come all this way just to meet with him. Yes, Doris decided. There was something about this man. She was still wondering where he'd come from, which gods might have sent him and to what end, when she had a sudden, terrible thought.

She sat up sharply.

'Is he the one who has taken the queen's throne? No. He can't be. My ma smiled at him, and she supports the queen. She'd hardly be smiling at someone who'd taken her friend's throne. Who *is* this mysterious queen, anyway? Where is she *now?* Will I *ever* meet her?'

Doris fell asleep, eventually, and had a snooze before setting off with Menander for a walk in the gardens. Once there, she trotted as far ahead as she dared so she could explore things on her own whilst still feeling safe. She wandered between statues and along marble colonnades, and was just about to chase a butterfly when she felt the ground tremble.

She paused.

She twitched an ear and listened.

There was definitely a rumble in the air.

She glanced over her shoulder, looking for Menander, but she couldn't see him. The rumble was getting louder, so she dived behind a pillar to hide, then edged back a little to keep an eye on the path she'd just left.

Now she could tell that the noise was pounding feet. Its volume increased still more, and a gang of men came into view. They were marching shoulder to shoulder, four abreast, and were wearing short leather skirts, bronze breastplates, and helmets with horsehair plumes. Each of them was carrying a heavy shield in one hand, a javelin in the other, and a sword and dagger at his waist. Their skin gleamed, their plumes swung backwards and forwards in time with their steps, and their armour glinted in the sunlight.

Doris's jaw dropped in awe.

'Who are *they*?' she muttered. 'What are they *doing* here? Does my ma know about this?'

She considered hightailing it back to the palace to warn Cleopatra about the men, but they were too close now. She didn't fancy her chances if they caught her.

Then she spotted something.

Encircled by the tanned and muscled bodies, and having to jog to keep up with them, was a pale and sickly-looking figure.

'That's Ptolemy,' Menander whispered from over her shoulder.

Doris gasped.

She recognised the name.

Cleopatra's advisors had talked about Ptolemy during their meetings at the merchant's house.

'He's your mistress's brother,' Menander explained. 'Don't be fooled by his size. He may be small, but he's been causing big problems. He and Cleopatra are supposed to rule Egypt together, as tradition holds. Unfortunately, they hate each other.'

Doris looked quizzically at Menander.

'Ptolemy and his sycophants raised an army against your mistress,' Menander continued. 'They made her quit her country and her throne...'

'Does that mean my *ma* is the *queen?*' Doris stamped her foot. 'Duh! Of *course* she is! Why didn't *I* think of that? It explains so many things. Now I understand why Menander treats me so *royally*...'

She straightened herself up and stuck her nose in the air.

'It's because am royal. I'm a *royal* dog!'

'Ptolemy may *look* pathetic,' said Menander, 'but he has tremendous support here in Alexandria. He's only thirteen, after all, so everyone thinks they can tell him what to do. They know very well they can't do that with your mistress.'

Doris giggled to herself.

Menander was right.

No one could tell Cleopatra what to do.

She glanced at Ptolemy's burly escorts and wondered who had given them their orders. Was someone trying to help her mistress at last? Why else would they be marching her troublesome brother about? Whatever the answers, she decided that the men posed no threat to her personally. Now she wanted to see where they were taking Ptolemy, and what would happen when they got him there.

She stayed still as a mouse until the rear of the escort drew level with her, then she sprang from her hiding place and ran as fast as she could.

'Doris!' Menander called. 'Come back, Doris!'

But Doris wasn't listening.

She streaked past the ranks of men until she reached their very front row. Then she settled herself alongside them as they marched straight through the palace doors.

The man who'd laughed was still there, but this time Cleopatra was right beside him. They were sitting on a pair of identical thrones which had been placed on a raised platform. Standing behind them was another man, a fan-waver. He was stripped to the waist and wore only a skimpy white linen skirt and golden cuffs around his arms and ankles. His fan was enormous, and was made of several peacock tails bound together on a long handle.

Positioned around the base of the platform was a group of handmaidens, including Charmion, and positioned around *them* were two plain pottery jars, a matching jug and a selection of wooden boards. Doris could see that the boards were loaded with hors d'oeuvres, including olives, pickled fish, asparagus, baby leeks and quails' eggs, plus bunches of grapes and slices of melon, apricot and papaya.

She was contemplating these delicious snacks and trying to decide which to head for first when Menander caught up with her. He crouched beside her and scolded her, rather halfheartedly, for running off.

'Do you see the wooden plates and pottery jars? How plain they are?' he asked. 'That is Ptolemy's doing. When our visitor arrived, Ptolemy had all the silver, gold and glass taken away and hidden. That's how petty he is.'

At that moment, Cleopatra laughed and reached for an olive, and Doris took a step forward to join her.

'Don't!' Menander urged as he grabbed her by the waist. 'Your mistress might *seem* happy and relaxed, but the mere mention of Ptolemy's name has been known to bring her out in a rash. Only the gods know what will happen now that she's face to face with him. Stay here with me, Doris, and watch from a distance.'

Ptolemy was still surrounded. His burly guards were packed so closely that all that Doris could see of him were his skinny ankles and the crisscrossed thongs of his leather sandals. The room was deathly quiet. Cleopatra leant back in her throne and rolled the olive in her mouth. When it burst with an audible pop, the man who'd laughed raised a hand and told the guards to move aside. Suddenly Ptolemy was standing alone in the middle of the room and looking smaller and paler than ever. He glanced at his sister and then at her guest, whom he seemed to recognise. Then he squirmed on the spot and turned green.

Doris now needed a better view of things so, despite

Menander's warning, she wriggled out of his grasp and trotted boldly across the room. But she didn't entirely ignore what Menander had said. Rather than jump onto Cleopatra's knee, she opted for the man who'd laughed instead. He looked a bit confused at first. He scrabbled to adjust his crumpled clothes, he touched an anxious hand to his laurel headdress but, when he found everything to his liking, he relaxed, pulled Doris closer to him and began to fiddle with her ears.

Doris's body slumped, her eyes glazed over and her chin nodded to her chest. She lay down and began to snuggle deeper into the man's lap. But no sooner had she found the perfect position than his voice boomed over her head and he *proclaimed,* no less, that Cleopatra and Ptolemy must patch up their differences and rule Egypt together.

Whereupon Ptolemy burst into tears and ran out of the room.

'You see my problem...' said Cleopatra.

She snapped her fingers and a manservant appeared from the shadows.

'Bring the silver and glass out of storage,' she ordered. 'And get rid of *that.*'

She pointed distastefully at the wooden plates and pottery jars.

'But leave us some grapes,' she added.

She turned to the man who'd laughed.

'Normal service will be resumed by this evening,' she said. 'You have my promise on that. For you are Julius Caesar, and as such you deserve nothing but the best.

The *very* best.'

It was then that Doris realised what she'd done.

The man who'd laughed was none other than the all-conquering Roman hero who was worshipped as a god. This was the most terrifying man she'd never met. And yet she'd sat, uninvited, on his lap.

She wanted the earth to swallow her up.

She tried to make herself small. She tucked her legs and tail beneath her, shrank her head between her shoulder blades and buried her nose in her paws, but Julius Caesar simply laughed again, fondled her ears, and passed her a grape.

CHAPTER THREE

Bo's House, somewhere in England.
The 21st Century

More than two-thousand years later, another poodle, whose name was Bo, opened her eyes in a coal hole and blinked. A large black beetle, a scarab, was clambering up the wall beside her.

'I...oh!'

'What?' asked a concerned voice. 'What happened?'

'J-J-Julius. Julius Caesar,' Bo stammered. 'Julius Caesar's what happened.'

She turned and looked into her friend's eyes.

They were much larger and browner than her own. Hers were like shiny black buttons. His were like ripe conkers. They were warm and kind and easy to read. Sometimes they showed concern, sometimes sadness, sometimes puzzlement.

They were typical spaniel's eyes, but this was no typical spaniel.

This was Cavendish.

Bo had first met Cavendish during a storm. She'd been alone in the house and had rushed to the cellar to escape the thunder and lightning. She'd expected the cellar to be cool and dark, but a light had been shining out from under a door, a door she'd never seen before. She'd pushed the door open and discovered the coal hole. It had been flooded with the light, and Bo had had to blink away the brightness before looking around. The room had seemed empty but for a few old tins of paint in one corner and a heap of folded dust sheets in another. Just then though, Bo had heard a shuffling sound and the dust sheets had toppled sideways. More shuffling, and one of the dust sheets had risen and fallen as if it were breathing. Bo had wanted to run for her life, but she'd found she couldn't move, even as something edged towards her.

That something had been Cavendish.

In those first few moments, he'd appeared as little more than a husk. His three-hundred-and-fifty-year-old body had not survived the early, experimental days of taxidermy, and his once plump flesh and gleaming, chestnut-and-white coat had been withered and dried. But then something magical had happened. Strange forces had breathed new life into the spaniel's empty veins and he'd come alive again. The rest, as they say, is history.

Cavendish had explained that he and Bo had once belonged to King Charles I of England, Scotland and Ireland. Bo had been called Mignonne in those days, and she and Cavendish had been the best of friends.

Bo had taken some convincing, but eventually she'd learnt to trust Cavendish. She'd confirmed for herself that present time stood still, or almost still, whilst they were together. She'd also learnt that she had a rare and extraordinary talent, a gift. She was able to time travel. She could go back to the days of King Charles, revisit her old life as Mignonne and see the many amazing things that Mignonne had seen. And that's exactly what she'd done. Yet, just when she'd thought her travels were over, Cavendish had revealed another surprise. He'd told Bo that he believed her gift was not just extraordinary, but extra special. He'd said that he thought she could choose any place and time in history, and if a poodle or poodle ancestor had been there, then she could become that dog.

It was Cavendish who'd suggested that Bo visit Egypt in Cleopatra's time. He'd pointed out the scarab beetle scrambling up the wall and said that the Egyptians had worshipped its very sort, and that that must be a good sign. He'd also said there'd be no mistaking the queen.

Well, he'd been wrong about that.

Bo had managed to travel back two-thousand years and become Doris the poodle puppy, but she'd had no idea that the young woman with the big smile and the oversized dog collar was the queen herself.

And since Cavendish had an irritating knack of being right about most things, Bo intended to press the point.

'J-Julius. Julius Caesar,' she stammered again.

'Tell me what happened,' Cavendish repeated. 'Are you saying you didn't meet Cleopatra?'

'No. I did meet her. But I didn't realise who she was. Not immediately, anyway.'

'Tell me.'

'Well,' Bo continued gleefully. 'For the first few days I just knew her as Cleopatra. I didn't know she was *that* Cleopatra. She was very young and quite giggly, and not like a queen at all.'

Cavendish smiled.

'I think I've got the message. I was wrong. Now please get on with the story.'

'I was very small. Just a pup, really. A lovely person called Menander took me to a palace, but then, after a couple of days, I was sent to the middle of nowhere. That's when I met Cleopatra.'

'She was in exile?'

'Yes. She'd lost her throne and gone away to hide. But I didn't know that then...'

Bo opened her eyes wide.

'She and I were *smuggled!*' she whispered conspiratorially. 'We were taken to a big ship and it sailed us to Alexandria, but then all its lights were put out and we were rowed into a harbour in the dark. Then we were rolled up in a carpet and *smuggled* into our palace. When we got there, Julius Caesar was waiting for us.'

'Is that what frightened you?'

'No. The frightening bit came later.'

'Did you see Cleopatra's brother?'

'Pale and sickly Ptolemy? Yes.'

'He was the reason you had to arrive in secret,' Cavendish explained. 'If he'd known that Cleopatra was home, he'd have had her murdered.'

'His own sister?'

'His own sister.'

'I know they hated each other,' said Bo, 'but I didn't know it was *that* bad. Caesar told them they must rule Egypt together. They seemed to listen. But then I suppose they would, wouldn't they. Caesar was an all-conquering hero.'

'Caesar had good reason to make them listen. Most of Egypt's neighbours were Roman territories, and it was Egypt who usually supplied their grain. But there'd been a bad drought. The harvests were paltry, grain was precious and Caesar needed what little there was. He needed to feed his *own* soldiers, not Ptolemy's and Cleopatra's. That's why he tried to bring them together. He did it for grain.'

'He laughed when Cleopatra and I rolled out of the carpet,' said Bo.

'I'm not surprised. That trick of Cleopatra's was clever, witty and brave. She got herself straight to Caesar's feet before Ptolemy even knew she was back. Caesar appreciated that, but it might have gone the other way. He might have reacted differently. He hadn't got where he was without being absolutely ruthless when it suited him.'

Bo trembled.

'Ruthless?' she repeated hoarsely. 'I hadn't thought of that. I knew he was powerful but then I sat on his knee without being asked. *That's* what frightened me. I sat on his knee before I realised who he was. He fed me a grape.'

'Then think yourself lucky. He obviously liked you.

Don't eat too many grapes, though. They're poisonous to dogs.'

Bo gulped.

'Caesar was trying to poison me?'

'No!' Cavendish laughed. 'Not many people know you can kill a dog with grapes. I doubt Caesar was one of them. And he had far more important things to think about than doing away with small poodles.'

'Don't tease me,' Bo sighed. 'He was the most powerful man in the world. Even I knew that. Everyone did. He could have had me thrown to the lions.'

Cavendish paused.

'Lions?' he repeated. 'Did you see lions?'

'Of course not!' Bo snorted. 'Don't be ridiculous! That's just a figure of speech.'

She hesitated.

'It is, isn't it?'

Cavendish changed the subject.

'What was your name in Egypt?' he asked.

Bo scratched her ear and pretended not to have heard.

'Bo?'

'Sorry?'

'I asked you what your name was. In Egypt.'

'Mmm...do you know, I don't think it was ever mentioned...'

'Don't be ridiculous. Tell me.'

'Doris,' Bo replied quietly. 'It was Doris.'

'*Doris?*'

'Yes. What's wrong with that?'

'Nothing,' said Cavendish. 'It's very charming.'

'It's Greek, actually,' said Bo defensively. 'Menander told me that. He's Cleopatra's Keeper of The Bedchamber. He said that Cleopatra's family were originally from Greece and that they didn't have a drop of Egyptian blood. Not one. Even Alexandria was Greek. It was built by Alexander the Great.'

'Yes, I did know that. Thank you, Bo.'

'Shall I go and see Cleopatra again?' Bo asked.

But Cavendish seemed a little distracted.

'Doris, Doris,' he muttered under his breath.

'Tomorrow then,' Bo sighed.

She glanced at the black beetle. It was clambering over and over. Time replayed the last few seconds of itself when Bo and Cavendish were together. As soon as Bo left the coal hole, time would move on, and so would the beetle.

'I'll do it tomorrow,' she said. 'When that beetle's gone.'

CHAPTER FOUR

The Royal Palace, Alexandria, Egypt.
December 48BC

Doris stood on her hind legs and put her front paws on the window sill. The marble was crudely cut and unpolished, but that didn't matter to Doris. The sill was now part of her life.

Despite Caesar's best efforts, Ptolemy and Cleopatra had fallen out again and their joint rulership had collapsed into war. Caesar had taken Cleopatra's side, but they were badly outnumbered. Caesar had only four-thousand soldiers in Egypt, whereas Ptolemy had more than five times that many. What's more, the citizens of Alexandria had turned against Cleopatra and her Roman friend and had surrounded the palace, trapping the queen and Doris inside it.

It was at that point that a royal stonemason, whose name was Serapion, had had a brilliant idea. He'd sat down with Cleopatra, Doris and Caesar, and shown them some drawings of the palace.

'If the worst happens,' he'd said, 'and the mob gets through, then Your Highnesses must have somewhere to hide. Somewhere where they can't find you and won't even think to look. I believe I've found that place.'

He'd tapped at the drawings with his index finger.

'It's just here, under the eaves. I could lay a floor and build a hidden entrance and stairway. I think it will make a fine room. I could even remove some sections of wall...here, here and here, and put in some windows to give Your Highnesses light and air. The area is too high above ground level for anyone to notice the changes. They won't know what I've done, and you'll be safe.'

'Better still,' Caesar had added as he put an arm round Cleopatra's shoulder, 'the windows will give you and Doris a view. You'll be able to keep an eye on the harbour and see all the way to the lighthouse.'

Cleopatra had nodded.

'Your idea is a good one, Serapion,' she'd said. 'But what about the palace? It isn't going to collapse, is it? I mean, if you start removing blocks of stone...'

Serapion had looked hurt.

'Your Highness...' he'd begun.

Then he'd seen the sparkle in Cleopatra's eyes.

'Start immediately,' she'd said, and within a matter of days she and Doris had been installed in the new room.

It had everything they needed to make them comfortable, including couches to lie on, tables to eat at, and ample supplies of food, water and wine. There were lanterns, candles and tapers and, just in case, a bed for the queen and Doris, and mattresses for their servants. So far, though, Doris and Cleopatra had only had to spend the daylight hours in their hidden bolt-hole, and had always returned to the palace at night, when Caesar got home from the fighting.

Doris shuffled along the sill and stared across the Royal Harbour to its big brother, the Great Harbour. She wanted to check the Egyptian ships and make sure they were still safe. She made this check four or five times a day. It was her way of trying to help her mistress and master. If she saw any strange movement in the harbour, or any change in the ships, she barked until someone came to join her at the window. So far, they'd just patted her on the head and asked her to be quiet.

She knew the ships were important. She knew that should Ptolemy's supporters ever get hold of them, Caesar and Cleopatra would be in real trouble. The ships would be run out to sea where they'd cut off Caesar's supplies, including the extra soldiers he'd ordered. If that happened, the game would most probably be over. Ptolemy would win the war, Caesar would be murdered and everyone would come looking for Doris and Cleopatra. Ptolemy's soldiers would break into the palace. They'd draw their swords, slash down the woollen curtains and overturn the furniture. They'd overturn everything. They'd turn the palace upside down. They'd hunt down their quarry until they found them, cornered and helpless and then... then...

Doris shivered at the thought.

'I'm not going to think about that now,' she muttered. 'I *can't* think about it. I'm on ship watch.'

She gazed ahead. The seventy-two vessels of the

31

Egyptian fleet were sitting together on the glittering harbour waters. Everything was calm. She began to turn and was just about to hop to the floor when a tiny movement caught her eye. She craned her neck and leant dangerously out of the window. Far below her, something was happening in the Royal Harbour. Caesar's own ships were being rowed away from their moorings and out towards a small island.

She barked.

'Shhht, Doris,' Cleopatra hushed her.

She barked again.

This time, Cleopatra glanced up.

'Doris! What are you *doing?* You'll *fall*!'

The queen sprang from her couch and rushed across the room.

'Don't lean out of the window like that!' she shrieked as she slipped a hand under Doris's collar. 'It's *very* dangerous and it scares me. What are you barking at?'

She looked over Doris's shoulder.

'Caesar is moving his ships,' the queen whispered. 'He said he might. He's decided he can no longer leave the Egyptian fleet unguarded. Ptolemy might seize it. If he did that, we'd be in real trouble.'

'Yes, ma,' Doris sighed. 'I know that. It's why I've been watching.'

'Caesar's men will round that little island so no one can see them,' the queen explained, 'then they'll row swiftly into the Great Harbour. Once there, they'll board the Egyptian ships and take control of them.'

The queen made a little gulping noise and Doris

twisted round to look at her. Tears were streaming down her face.

'I know I'm being silly, Doris,' Cleopatra sniffed. 'This is war, and Caesar's only doing what he must. But the men on those ships are true sailors, my country's sailors. They are not trained to fight on deck, as Romans are. Caesar's soldiers will rush aboard with daggers drawn and the sailors won't know *what* to do. Caesar thinks they'll surrender quickly. I hope he's right.'

She wiped her cheeks with the heel of her hand and lifted Doris clear of the window.

'Menander will be here soon. When he comes, we will ask him to pull up some chairs, and then we will all sit and watch together.'

By the time Menander had seated Cleopatra and himself, and pulled Doris onto his knee, the Roman rowers had reached the Egyptian fleet. It was hard to see exactly what was going on, but there wasn't much noise either, so Cleopatra soon decided that the Romans had succeeded in capturing the ships without too much bloodshed.

'It is done,' she laughed. 'We have secured the fleet! Now we can be at rest. Come. Shall we have something to eat?'

She stood up and turned to push her chair away from the window.

'No, wait!' Doris barked.

Something was tickling her nose.

She could smell smoke.

'Mistress?' Menander asked in a shaky voice. 'What's

that, mistress?'

His right arm was pointing straight out in front of him, towards a flicker of orange light. Within seconds, the flicker had spread into a line of flames and there was a whoosh as the flames shot high in the air and became a towering wall of fire and cinder.

'The gods!' Cleopatra gasped. 'He's torched it! Caesar has torched the Egyptian fleet!'

The fire was raging so fiercely now that Doris could feel its heat on her face. Flakes of ash were fluttering through the window and landing on her fur, and a pillar of smoke was rising out of the Great Harbour and drilling into the sky.

'*Why?*' Cleopatra wailed. 'Why set fire to those beautiful ships?'

She sank to her knees and sobbed.

'Don't cry, ma,' Doris whimpered. 'I'm sure Caesar has his reasons. I'm sure he knows what he's doing.'

Later, when Doris and Cleopatra had almost finished their dinner, an intruder came up the secret stairs. He was grey as a ghoul and cloaked in the acrid smell of burning.

Doris growled, shrank from Cleopatra's knee and hid herself under a chair.

'Don't you recognise him?' Cleopatra laughed. 'Don't you see who it is?'

'No,' Doris barked. 'No, I don't.'

Doris watched from the safety of the chair as the ghoul and his armour clanked towards her. She trembled as he knelt down, and then sighed with relief as he laid his sword aside. He leant inward and, as he wiped the ash from his face, Doris recognised the tanned flesh and beady black eyes of her master. She ran into his arms and Caesar laughed and stood up.

'I'm sorry about the ships, my love,' he told the queen. 'I had to set fire to them. I had no choice. We captured them easily enough, but then I realised that holding onto them would be a full time job. I don't have enough soldiers for that.'

He reached out and took hold of one of Cleopatra's hands.

'Do you see?' he asked.

The queen nodded, pushed a glass of wine towards him and tore him a hunk of bread.

'Sit,' she said. 'Eat. We can get more. We can ask the kitchens...'

'No,' Caesar replied. 'I have no appetite, but I do have news, *good* news...'

He paused for effect.

'Well?' Cleopatra urged him. 'What? Tell us, Julius! Don't keep us in suspense...'

'That was *some* fire!' Caesar exclaimed. 'Did you see it?'

'Yes, yes. We saw it. But what? What is your news?'

'Everybody was distracted by it. The air was thick with smoke. No one could see anything...'

'*And?*'

'And so we took our chance. We stormed the Pharos, my darling. We took it from under the enemy's nose! We hold the Pharos! We hold the gateway to all of Egypt and the Mediterranean!'

This was a major coup. No one could navigate the approach to Alexandria without guidance from the great lighthouse. Now Caesar had taken it over, the threat to the Egyptian fleet was gone, and it seemed that Caesar's luck was beginning to turn. He threw back his head and laughed, and Cleopatra and Doris squealed with delight.

CHAPTER FIVE
The Royal Palace, Alexandria, Egypt.
February 47BC

There was an island next to the lighthouse, and this island was joined to Alexandria by a causeway, the Heptastadion. Caesar now decided to block this causeway off so that Ptolemy couldn't use it to re-take the lighthouse.

The work was about to begin and, as Caesar and his men headed out, Doris and Cleopatra raced up the secret steps to their eyrie and made straight for the window nearest the Heptastadion. They soon spotted Caesar, but they had to concentrate hard. The Heptastadion was a fair way off, and the glare from the sunlight on the harbour made their eyes water.

The Romans had brought ships alongside to protect the soldiers whilst they worked, and all was going to plan when, to Cleopatra and Doris's horror, a stream of enemy troops leapt onto the causeway.

'Look behind you!' Cleopatra shrieked.

'Run! Run!' barked Doris.

Caesar couldn't hear the warning, of course, and by the time he'd spotted the ambush, it was too late. He and his men were stranded. Their only way out was to jump into the water or board the ships, but if *they* could do that, then so could the enemy. The ships' rowers had realised this and had already begun to move away. When the soldiers saw what was happening, they panicked. Few of them could swim, so they flung themselves at the ships, hoping to scramble into them. Some fell straight into the water, others made it, but then unbalanced the ships, which began to sink. Stones and arrows hailed down from the Egyptian slingers and archers, and the waters churned with screaming, flailing men and swishing oars.

It was mayhem.

'Where's Caesar?' Cleopatra cried. 'I can't find him, Doris. I can't see him!'

'I can!' Doris barked.

It was true. Doris hadn't once lost sight of her master.

She could see him *very* clearly.

'He's over there, ma. He's safe! He's on one of the ships! Oh!'

Whilst Doris had been watching, more soldiers had poured onto the vessel.

'Surely that's too many people,' she mumbled. 'I don't think it can take that many...'

The ship began to lurch, but Doris kept her eyes glued on Caesar. He had a roll of papers in one hand. Doris could see him holding them above his head. Then he held his nose and jumped overboard.

'He's swimming, ma, he's swimming!'

Caesar was wearing full armour, including back and

breast plates, shin guards, arm cuffs and a helmet, and the weight was soon dragging him down. What's more, he seemed determined to keep his papers dry, so he was swimming with only one arm. Every so often, he went under, and Doris had to watch the papers bob along the surface until he emerged again. Cleopatra had given up trying to find him by then and was pacing the room.

'Please,' she prayed aloud. 'Please bring him home to us. I'll do anything, just don't let him drown.'

Then Doris lost sight of him, too.

Hours passed, and Cleopatra continued to pace up and down. She'd cuddle Doris close, then put her on the couch. She'd walk backwards and forwards and pray. She'd pick Doris up again, return to the window and look across the harbour to the capsized ships and floating bodies. Then she'd pray some more. Every so often, there'd be a noise far below in the palace, and she and Doris would start in expectation.

Still there was no news.

Then, at long last, there was the sound of familiar footsteps, and Charmion came hurtling up the secret stairs.

'Mistress! Mistress!' she screamed.

Cleopatra's face turned ashen.

'Tell me quick,' she said. 'For I know it is bad.'

Charmion hesitated.

'Mistress, he...'

There was a clatter and more footsteps,

'So! Where are my girls?' bellowed Caesar.

He was soaking wet.

His helmet and shield were clamped under one arm and he was holding the other aloft.

'Papers,' he said. 'Very important papers. *Almost* dry.'

CHAPTER SIX
The Royal Palace, Alexandria, Egypt.
March 47BC

Caesar's extra troops had arrived at last. Ptolemy had drowned in The Nile whilst trying to escape, and his army had been defeated. Caesar was victorious, Cleopatra was the sole and undisputed ruler of Egypt, and Doris was about to celebrate.

Menander had given her a rose petal and jasmine scented bath and conditioned her coat with his homemade concoction of pistachio and pomegranate.

'There,' he'd said as he'd wrapped her in a hot towel. 'Let that soak in nicely whilst I see to your mistress.'

Now, four hours later, he was back.

'The queen is almost ready,' he told Doris as he rinsed off the conditioner. 'She is looking beautiful. More beautiful than ever. And so will you, when I've finished with you. For this is a very important day. There will be a parade, and a big party. You've never been to one of Cleopatra's parties have you? Just you wait. It'll be a night to remember.'

Doris wagged her tail and Menander dried her fur, teased out the knots and trimmed her ears into perfect triangles. Then he slipped golden cuffs onto her ankles and spiralled her tail with golden cord. Finally, he positioned and fixed her headdress. This was also made of gold, though it was hollow rather than solid. Solid gold would have been too heavy for Doris. She wouldn't have been able to lift her head.

The headdress was made to look like cobras wreathing through sheaves of corn. The very front of it, the part which sat just above Doris's eyes, had a mirrored disc made from highly polished silver. It was this disc, a representation of the moon, that set the headdress apart, for only two earthly beings had the right to wear it - Doris and Cleopatra herself.

As a final touch, Menander attached a string of pearls to the cord on Doris's tail.

'Come,' he said, holding the pearls like a lead. 'Let's find your mistress.'

Menander took Doris to a balcony which overlooked Alexandria's central street, the Canopic.

The balcony had been swagged with purple silk and flowers. Garlands of laurel and jasmine had been twisted around its pillars, and there were huge potted palms on its marble floor. Handmaidens and fan-wavers stood about it in picturesque groups, and flute-players trilled soothing tunes.

Seated in the balcony's centre, on a carved and gilded throne, was Cleopatra. Next to her was a miniature version of the same throne, and Menander lifted Doris onto this, laid her on her back, and propped her up with cushions. Her chest and tummy pointed skyward, her hind legs were spread-eagled, and her front paws rested on the throne's arms.

'There,' said Menander, 'so beautiful you look.'

'She does indeed,' Cleopatra agreed. 'But take your place quickly, Menander. The parade is about to begin.'

Menander bowed and walked backwards to his spot behind the queen's throne, and Doris took a sideways glance at her mistress and gulped.

Doris had never seen Cleopatra in full regalia. In the six months they'd known each other, there'd been no opportunity for dressing-up, and so Doris had become used to seeing her mistress wearing simple, Grecian-style garments. Her hairstyle was usually simple too, with soft curls around her face and neck and a plaited bun at the back of her head. Even her jewellery had been plain. She rarely wore more than a golden headband, pearl earrings and a snake-headed bangle.

Today, however, she was sporting something else entirely.

The costume of the ancient Egyptian goddess Isis was one of unashamed drama and glamour, yet it was no mere fancy dress outfit. The Egyptians believed that any queen of theirs *was* Isis and, at important occasions such as this, the goddess was expected to come down to earth and make a personal appearance. Cleopatra was therefore dressed as the embodiment of The Supreme Goddess Of The Moon And The Great Mother Of All The Gods And Of Nature.

Everything Isis wore related to nature, but the single most telling item was the mirrored disc in the centre of her forehead. This was her distinguishing feature and, like Doris's much smaller version, it represented the moon. The rest of Cleopatra's headdress was like Doris's, too, except that in the queen's case the cobras and sheaves of corn were studded with precious stones and wrought from solid, rather than hollow, gold. Her gown had been made to illustrate the sun and earth. Its linen fabric, so fine as to be virtually transparent, had been dyed in all the pinks and reds of dawn and then embroidered with exotic birds, fruit and flowers. Her cloak was of black silk spangled with a thousand tiny stars, just like the night sky, and her hair was dressed with false plaits and ringlets which tumbled over her shoulders. Her lips had been tinted glossy red, and her eyelids shimmered with iridescent green malachite outlined in black kohl.

Doris swallowed hard.

Her mistress looked incredible, beautiful, out of this world - and absolutely terrifying.

The scared young woman whom Doris had first met at a merchant's house in a remote village seemed long gone, but Doris knew differently. The twenty-three-year-old queen might have proved herself to be ambitious and clever, but she was still gentle and kind. She still played childish practical jokes and collapsed into fits of the giggles. She still sent for Doris in the middle of the night, cuddled her close and sang lullabies in myriad languages. To Doris, Cleopatra was nothing more nor less than her wonderful, loving ma.

The queen caught Doris's eye and winked, and Doris barked in reply, then gingerly shifted her attention back to the Canopic. She didn't want to dislodge her headdress and have it slip over one eye just as Caesar was about to arrive.

That would be very embarrassing indeed.

She hitched herself up on her cushions and peered over the top edge of the balcony. Beyond the swags of silk and the garlands of flowers, the Canopic stretched ahead of her. It was a wide, straight avenue, so long that Doris couldn't see its end. All along it, ranks of Roman soldiers were standing to attention in the sun and holding back the crowds. Doris half-closed her eyes and the soldiers fuzzed into two parallel lines of silver-scarlet ribbons. They were almost motionless. Only the occasional glint of armour or the flutter of a red woollen cloak or horse hair plume gave them away as living people. Doris didn't know how they managed to stand so still.

The heat was stifling.

Cleopatra's perfect skin was glowing prettily, but Doris, being a dog, wasn't able to sweat, and could only cool herself by spreading herself about and panting. She knew this wasn't very attractive, but she didn't have an option. Charmion and the other handmaidens were doing their best. They were wafting her with palm fronds and sprinkling her with rose-water, but none of it seemed to help.

Doris was beginning to think she might melt.

When she heard the rumble of distant hooves, she

drummed her heels on her cushions.

'Something's happening, ma.'

'Now it begins,' Cleopatra whispered. 'Sit up straight my darling, and watch.'

From far, far away, the Roman outriders appeared.

Tiny at first, growing larger by the second, their magnificent white horses galloped flat out along the Canopic and straight towards the balcony. Doris watched them thunder over the paving stones. She watched the horses' nostrils flaring red as sweat darkened their pounding chests and misted around them in clouds. They were coming so fast that Doris was afraid they wouldn't be able to stop and might crash into the wall below her. But stop they did, before lining up in front of her.

Then came the next onslaught, a legion of Roman soldiers, twenty abreast. They held their standards aloft and marched with such fierce pride that Doris was sure she could feel the city shake. Eventually, they too, took their places and stood still and silent.

On and on it went until the widest avenue in the world was packed to bursting with men and horses and only a single, central path remained.

Then everything went quiet. Nobody moved a muscle. It seemed to Doris that the whole world was holding its breath until, somewhere at the very furthest end of the city, a trumpet sounded.

Horns wailed, cymbals crashed, drums rolled, but all was drowned to nothing by the roars of the crowd. Millions of streamers and flower petals were tossed in the air, and Doris had to narrow her eyes to peer through the dizzying blizzard. There was a blur of silk and a whirr of wheels, the crowd erupted into a final frenzy, and Doris's jaw dropped wide open.

Hurtling towards her was the most incredible sight she'd ever seen.

Julius Caesar, her hero and master, was standing upright on a golden chariot. His purple cloak was streaming out behind him and his brown arms were thrust forward and straining at the reins of the six mighty animals who were drawing him at full speed along the Canopic. They were close, now. Their manes were rising and falling, thumping against their shoulders with each long, bouncing stride. Their ears were pinned back and their noses were pink with exertion as their giant paws softly ate up the ground.

Doris closed her eyes.

'I imagined that,' she muttered.

Then she looked again.

'Oh dear. I didn't. Those really *are* lions.'

CHAPTER SEVEN
Later that day

Doris was back in her salon. She'd had a long, cold shower and *almost* got over the shock of the lions. Now something else was worrying her. Menander was about to arrive to get her ready for Cleopatra's party. She could hear his footsteps in the corridor outside. She glanced over at the cobra and corn sheaf headdress. It was a beautiful thing, but when Menander had removed it after the parade and put it on its golden hat stand, Doris had been left with squashed ears and a thumping headache. The last thing she wanted was to do now was to put the headdress on again, but she had a horrible feeling she might have to.

Menander came through the door, but Doris didn't leap up to welcome him as she usually did. Instead, she laid her nose on her paws and looked at him mournfully.

Menander laughed.

'Don't worry,' he said as he withdrew something from behind his back. 'Look at this!'

He held up a circlet of citrus blossom.

'I made it myself,' he said. 'I picked the blossom this morning, in the gardens. I knew you wouldn't enjoy the party in that heavy headdress.'

Doris sighed. It was typical of Menander to be so thoughtful. She couldn't believe she'd thought he'd be anything else. She jumped enthusiastically onto her stool in front of the mirror and Menander selected a brush and set about fluffing up her fur.

Doris always enjoyed these moments with Menander. Of all Cleopatra's many servants, he was Doris's favourite by far. Perhaps it went back to that very first day, when he'd collected her from her mother and taken her through the streets of Alexandria to the palace, but Doris didn't think so. She thought she'd have loved him whatever the circumstances.

Doris realised that Menander was what they called a eunuch. She wasn't exactly sure what 'eunuch' meant, but there were plenty of them at the palace and they were very distinctive. They all had high, singsong voices and wore extravagant make-up, sparkling jewellery and ladies' dresses. Doris thought they were probably from some sort of exotic tribe.

After an hour or so of careful fluffing, Menander was happy with Doris's coat but, just as he was about to lower the circlet onto her head, he paused halfway, leant close and whispered in her ear.

'Don't let this ruin your day,' he confided, 'but you have a visitor.'

Doris looked up.

Sure enough, another of the eunuchs was leaning against the salon's doorframe. He had a petulant sneer on his face, and his arms and ankles were crossed in an arrogant manner.

His name was Polygnotus, and Doris hated him even more than she loved Menander.

She hated his hennaed hair, his vulgar clothes and his heavy perfume. She loathed his thin lips, his plucked and pencilled eyebrows, his spidery hands and his narrow nose with its bulbous end. Most of all, she despised his spiteful, vicious nature and the way he was always trying to wheedle himself into Cleopatra's favour.

'The queen has asked me to escort Doris to this evening's celebrations,' said Polygnotus smugly.

'So I hear,' Menander replied with a wink to Doris.

They both knew that Polygnotus had only been given this honourable task by default. This was Cleopatra's first big party since her return from exile, and the first she'd ever thrown with Caesar as co-host. It was an incredibly important occasion, and the queen had asked for Menander's undivided attention throughout it all. That wasn't unusual in itself. Charmion often took responsibility for Doris if Menander was busy. But this party was dedicated to Isis, and since Charmion was Cleopatra's favourite handmaiden, and therefore that of the goddess, too, she had to wear a special costume and be present from the start. Which meant that someone else had had to be found to take Doris to the party. It could have been any one of a hundred people. It just so happened that of all the many things to be done that night, and of all the many servants available to do them, Polygnotus had drawn the 'Doris' straw. But he'd chosen not to notice that, such was his vanity.

'Well, make haste then,' he bossed. 'I'm missing the fun.'

'There *is* no fun 'til Doris arrives,' said Menander calmly.

He winked at Doris again and pinned the citrus blossom in place.

'*So* gorgeous!' he exclaimed. 'Off you go now, sweetie, have a lovely time.'

Doris flinched when Polygnotus picked her up. He didn't hold her close, as anyone else would have done. He thrust her at arm's length so she wouldn't crease his dress. Then he rushed her out of the salon and headed for the party.

Polygnotus may not have been nice, to put it mildly, but he was clever and ambitious and his scheming nature always gave him an eye for the main chance. He knew that all the dignitaries of Alexandria had been invited to the party, even those who'd plotted against Caesar and Cleopatra. They'd be waiting in line to fawn over their victorious hosts, and there'd be a long queue at the main entrance. So Polygnotus took the insiders' short-cut, through the palace kitchens.

When Cleopatra gave a party, no one ever knew when, or even if, she would give the word for dinner to be served. What *was* known, though, was that when the command came, the food must be perfect. It must be hot, freshly prepared and immaculately presented. The only way to ensure this was to cook and plate up each dish to perfection and hope it would be sent for within seconds of it being ready. If it wasn't, it was thrown away. This could happen over and over again until the queen decided that she and her guests were ready to eat. Sometimes she never did.

The kitchens that produced these meals were always incredibly noisy, humid with steam and hot from open fires, and this night was no different.

It was worse.

The menu was huge, there were hundreds of guests, and Cleopatra's hopes and expectations were higher than ever. By the end of the night, many thousands of dishes would need to be prepared. Exactly how many of those would avoid the bins and make it to the party was anybody's guess.

Doris and Polygnotus weaved their way between the open fires that smoked and spat and leapt up without warning in a whoosh of blue flames. Carcasses of exotic animals and birds were hanging by their feet from the ceiling, and rows of people were lowering them down and chopping them into cuts. Still more people were dicing vegetables, mixing herbs, grinding spices or polishing fruit. There were buckets of feathers, fur and peelings, and trays of all sorts of things at various stages of preparation. Everyone was sweating, and all of them seemed to be shouting or swearing at someone else, with one notable exception.

The queen's personal chef, Demetrius, was an elderly man who had served under her father, Ptolemy XII.

In his youth, Demetrius had gained a reputation for his fiery temper and cripplingly high standards. He had cursed his sous chefs, thrown well-aimed pans at them, and had even been known to hang them up from a meat hook by their apron strings to bring them into line. He'd taught knife-craft by making his trainees cut carrots, all night long if necessary, until the vegetables were as thin as horsehair. If he'd wanted to punish somebody, he'd given them a bamboo shoot to chew, then set them to scrubbing the floors with its frayed ends.

Now, though, Demetrius's years of teaching had paid off, his superb and trusted staff were the envy of the known world, and he could go about his work more quietly. He could enjoy planning his menus and taking time to research and find the rarest and tastiest ingredients for his unique recipes. He oversaw their preparation, of course, but he remained calm and unruffled. He'd given up the dramatics long ago. He'd seen it all before.

Polygnotus tried to scuttle past Demetrius and get straight to the party, but the old chef spotted Doris.

'Bring her to me!' he called across the room. 'And then stand away from the food. You should not be here, Polygnotus. I cannot allow untrained staff in my kitchen. You know how I feel about that. But bring Doris forward. I have a little tit-bit for her!'

Polygnotus couldn't ignore this summons. To do so would have been seen as a deliberate insult to the maestro, and therefore to the queen herself. Cleopatra would almost certainly get to hear about it, and

Polygnotus would probably be whipped. So Polygnotus did as he was told, but he was furious at being delayed, and made sure that Doris knew about it by pinching her vindictively. It didn't matter to Doris. A little nip from a nasty nobody was a small price to pay for her favourite treat. The fresh, honey-roasted dormouse was dripping with lavender and rosemary sauce, and Doris was still savouring its delicious aftertaste when Polygnotus hauled her out of the kitchens and made sure to pinch her again. Then, once inside the great reception hall, he dropped her to the floor, hastily brushed himself down, and pranced off to get as close to the action as possible.

Doris wasn't bothered. She was glad to be free of his hateful, spidery hands and his nasty secret nips. She knew that no one would blame her if she snapped at him, but she preferred not to lower herself. One day, someone - Menander perhaps - or better still, Cleopatra or Caesar, would catch him at it.

Then he'd get his comeuppance.

Meanwhile, Doris could make her way to the heart of the party. She'd be ushered straight to Cleopatra's innermost sanctum, whereas Polygnotus had no hope of getting within a cobra's spit of it.

Doris giggled with satisfaction and padded towards her mistress. Menander had been right. This *would* be a night to remember. Cleopatra's party was packed with glamorous people and intriguing sights and scents.

Perhaps it was the freshened incense, perhaps there were simply too many distractions. Whatever the reason,

Doris's acute sense of smell deserted her, and she failed to pick up one very singular and unusual aroma.

She rounded a marble statue and walked straight into a lion.

She froze.

The lion lifted its great head and circled its nose in the air.

Doris took four steps back.

The lion took one step forward.

There was a loud thwack and Doris realised with relief that the cat could come no further. It had reached the limit of a chain. It was tied to a pillar. The thwack, though, had alerted four of its friends, more lions, who suddenly appeared from behind more statues, sat down on their haunches, and stared.

For a while Doris could do no more than stare back.

Her eyes were about level with the lions' chests, which were draped in thick, chocolate-brown manes. She noticed the whorls of pale, creamy fur on their knees and legs, and the hugeness of their feet, which were planted on the floor like leaden dinner plates.

She didn't want to look at their faces.

She whimpered, and Cleopatra, who was sitting with Caesar on the far side of the beasts, called out to her.

'Have no fear, Doris,' the queen said calmly. 'For they are Caesar's cats alone and shall not harm you, by the Glory of Isis!'

On hearing that, the first lion retreated, his chain slackened, and he sat down with the others.

'*Doris*?' he intoned. 'Not Doris The Great Iwiw of

Isis?' he asked breathily. 'Not Doris Of The Lovely Hair?'

'The very same,' Doris replied rather more boldly than she'd intended.

All five lions then lowered their upper bodies to the floor and shuffled forward on their stomachs. They sniffed and grunted and dragged themselves closer with their claws, which slipped and skittered on the marble and made horrible squeaking noises.

Doris shuddered.

'I'm just Cleopatra's pet,' she added meekly.

At which point the lions rolled onto their backs and let their paws flop in the air.

Doris stood awhile and watched them. They'd spoken to her in Felcanish, the seldom-used language which cats and dogs share. She knew that that meant they weren't stupid, and wondered whether this was a good thing or not.

Not, she decided.

Seconds passed, though it seemed like hours.

Doris took a tentative step forward but none of the lions moved. They appeared to be in some sort of trance. Their eyes had rolled back in their sockets, and their bristly tongues were lolling out of the sides of their mouths. Doris could see saliva glistening on their dark gums and slithering over their big yellow teeth. She peered at their feet. The pads alone were bigger than the whole of one of her paws. The claws were retracted now, but they were still showing through the buff-coloured fur, and were hooked and sharp and strong as steel.

'Release them, Doris, Great Iwiw of Isis,' spoke Caesar suddenly. 'Grant them your most esteemed blessing.'

'Why bother?' Doris thought. 'And more to the point, what would be considered, in the eyes of five fully grown black-maned lions, an esteemed blessing as bestowed by a small poodle?'

Still, it was worth a try.

She stood on her hind legs and did a little dance, adding some interesting moves and a few quick, sharp barks of the sort she thought an 'iwiw', the Ancient Egyptian word for dog, might make.

The lions stirred.

Doris noticed then that Charmion was standing nearby. She was wearing her special 'handmaiden of Isis' costume and was using both hands to support a large basket that was resting on one of her shoulders. The basket was filled with an arrangement of fruit, flowers and sheaves of corn which had been wired together to make them look as though they were spilling onto the floor. Doris bounded up to the nearest sheaf, tore it away and returned to the lions. Then, with a furious shake of her head, she scattered their spotted stomachs with chaff.

That worked.

The lions sprang up and formed a line, then sat on their bottoms and stared at her with their moist yellow eyes.

'Aw,' Doris muttered, 'just like a basket of kittens. I *don't* think.'

A sixth lion appeared.

Doris hadn't noticed him before, but now he brushed past the others, even the first and biggest, and approached her directly. He reached the end of his chain, lowered his head and stroked the floor with the side of his face.

'Hail, Doris Of The Lovely Hair!' he purred, 'Most Esteemed And Greatest Iwiw of Isis The Goddess and Mother Of All The Gods And Of Nature. Hail! Pet Of Cleopatra Of Egypt, Revered Companion Of Julius Caesar The God Amon Incarnate, Divine Dog of...'

'All right, all right,' Doris replied. 'Doris is fine.'

'Cassius,' the lion introduced himself. 'My name is Cassius of Cyprus. Pleased to make your acquaintance this night.'

He raised a paw, and Doris raised one back.

'We are come from Rome,' the lion continued, 'to pull great Caesar's chariot.'

'Yes, I saw that,' Doris replied. 'Very impressive. Well, er, I'd best be off now. Nice to meet you. 'Bye.'

'Good bye,' said the lion. 'I hope we will meet again one day. In Rome, perhaps. All roads lead to Rome, you know.'

'Lovely,' mumbled Doris, shuffling sideways.

She was careful to stay out of the lions' reach until she was well beyond it. Then she trotted across the floor to Caesar and jumped gratefully onto his knee. He handed her a morsel of flamingo tongue and she chewed it pensively and looked back at the six cats. Their tails were swishing and their yellow eyes were glinting in the candlelight.

'Rome indeed,' she thought. 'Even now they're probably squabbling over who gets to eat my best bits. I know cats. They might be worshipped here in Egypt, but not by me.'

In Egypt the punishment for killing a cat was death.

Doris wondered if this applied to Cleopatra. She was Greek, after all, and the Greeks had a much healthier attitude to cats.

They ate them.

Though Doris thought that probably didn't include lions.

CHAPTER EIGHT
Bo's House.
The 21st Century

'You're trembling,' said Cavendish when Bo got back to the coal hole. 'What happened *this* time? Was it Caesar again? Surely not. Doris must have made friends with him by now.'

'*Big* friends,' Bo nodded. 'Caesar and Doris are *big* friends. No. It wasn't him...'

She paused for maximum effect.

'...it was his *lions*!'

'Caesar's lions?'

'Yes.'

'They're fine,' said Cavendish with a dismissive wave of his paw.

Bo found Cavendish very exasperating, sometimes.

'Oh, *really*!' she retorted. 'And what do *you* know about lions, *exactly*? You've probably never even *seen* a lion...and I go walking into, not one, but six of the things...'

'As a matter of fact...'

But there was no stopping Bo.

'You think you know everything, Cavendish. But

turning a corner and walking into lions - that's not funny. They're cats and they're huge, and they have big yellow teeth with eyes to match, and feet like dinner plates with claws on the end, and they, well, they *eat* things they *shouldn't*. Things like poodles.'

'Well Caesar's lions didn't. They were pets,' said Cavendish calmly. 'The Romans collected exotic pets. They were always catching strange beasts in foreign lands and taking them back to Rome. I remember a giraffe caused a bit of a stir. *Heard*,' he added quickly, 'I *heard* about it.'

'Cleopatra collected exotic *people*,' said Bo, who hadn't noticed Cavendish's slip-up. 'Eunuchs, they're called. They're *very* exotic. They come from a special tribe. Menander's one of them.'

'Eunuchs weren't from a tribe, Bo.'

'They must have been. They weren't like anyone else, only each other. They were tall but they had high voices and wore floaty frocks and spangly jewelry.'

'That doesn't prove they were related. Ideally, they weren't related to anybody. That was the whole point. They were taken from their families when they were small, and...'

Cavendish screwed up his nose and winced.

'...castrated.'

'You mean like people do to boy dogs so they can't make puppies?' asked Bo.

'Similar,' Cavendish replied with a peevish look. 'It's a similar thing. It made the eunuchs safe. It meant they could work for important women and do all the bedroomy things like bathing them and dressing their hair without fear of unwanted...puppies. Some eunuchs made gentle and devoted servants.'

'That sounds like Menander,' said Bo affectionately. 'He's *very* gentle and devoted.'

'Others were more ambitious. Being surrounded by people of power and wealth had a bad effect on them. They became jealous and scheming.'

'And *that* sounds like Polygnotus,' Bo added with a shiver. 'He's a *reptile*.'

'Ah, well, don't worry. He'll soon be among friends.'

'How so?'

'Ever heard of crocodiles?' Cavendish asked.

Bo nodded.

'Yes,' she said. 'I've seen them on TV.'

'Well, Egypt has big crocodiles. Nile crocodiles are some of the biggest reptiles in the world.'

'Lovely,' said Bo. 'But what's that got to do with Polygnotus?'

'Cleopatra took Doris and Caesar on a Nile cruise...'

'On a boat?' Bo asked. 'I hope it was on a boat...'

Cavendish tipped his head.

'A boat?' he considered. 'No. I don't think that's *quite* the word for it.'

CHAPTER NINE
Cleopatra's State Barge, The River Nile, Egypt.
Spring 47BC

Cleopatra's State Barge was no ordinary boat. It was a floating palace, a massive vessel with fabulous court rooms, bedchambers and salons. Its decks were landscaped with gardens, pebbled pathways and marble colonnades, and real grass and plants grew between its statues, ponds and fountains.

It was like a home from home, and Doris loved it.

She'd also taken up a new hobby, which she called 'crocodile spotting'.

This involved lying on the barge's upper deck, pushing her nose and front paws under its side rails, and watching the riverbank roll slowly by until she 'spotted' her quarry. Then she'd stand up and bark before lying down and starting all over again. The crocodiles were always there, but picking them out from their surroundings took patience and practice. Doris soon became an expert. She could find them dozing in the shade of papyrus plants, sunning themselves on sandy beaches, or slipping silently into the cool water. They looked lazy, but Doris had seen for herself what effective killing machines they were.

She'd seen how swiftly they could whip into action. Those heavy, cumbersome bodies were deceptively long-legged and quick on land, but they were decidedly lethal in water. They could leap vertically out of the shallows. Doris had seen that for herself. She'd watched a lone croc streak out of nowhere, clamp its ragged teeth onto a full-grown buffalo and drag it under. There'd been no trace of the buffalo but for a few bubbles floating on the surface.

Doris had been both appalled and fascinated. She hardly dared imagine what might have happened if there'd been more than one of the beasts. They'd probably have fought over the poor buffalo and torn him apart between them.

One morning, the crocodile spot was interrupted by a sudden shout and the boom of a gong. Someone had ordered the barge to be stopped. Doris dug her front claws into the decking and leant as far over its side as she dared. Far below her, the vessel's hundred or so oars were protruding from its hull like the legs of a giant centipede. Doris watched their solid silver blades flip and turn, then brake mid-swish and rise out of the river. The barge slowed to a near standstill and there was another shout.

Doris got up and ran towards it.

When she arrived at the barge's stern, she saw that one of its many escort ships had pulled alongside. These escort ships were loaded with many different things. Caesar had brought hundreds of his own soldiers, advisors and supplies with him, and Cleopatra never travelled light.

As well as a huge human entourage, the ships carried crates of spare furniture, musical instruments and costumes, plus the more mundane basics like food and water. Transfers were a daily event, but they usually took place at dusk or dawn, and that morning's delivery had already been made.

Even so, it looked as though something was coming aboard. There was a huddle of officers and a line of slaves on the decks of both ships, and the officers were leaning over the gap between them and discussing something in earnest. After a few minutes, they seemed to reach a decision, and there was a rush of activity as they shouted commands. The slaves began unravelling ropes and lowering a gangplank, and Doris sat down bemusedly and watched.

A large box was wheeled onto the deck of the escort ship. It was shrouded in linen sheeting and had sturdy ropes tied to its top corners. A burly slave on the escort ship took a firm grip of two of these ropes and tossed the others to his equally burly counterpart on the barge. Meanwhile, more slaves began to push the box forward on its wheel carriage and line it up with the gangplank.

Doris sighed.

'This had better be good,' she mumbled.

She glanced at the barge's officers who were monitoring proceedings. They were looking very nervous. Some of them were opening and closing their fists. Others seemed to be twitching.

'Grief!' thought Doris. 'What on earth is *in* that thing?'

Finally, the box was manoeuvred onto the gangplank and pushed towards the barge. There was a nasty moment when a front wheel slipped and the box lurched dangerously towards the river. Everybody gasped, but the burly slaves tugged hard on the safety ropes and managed to hoist the box free just as the wheel carriage fell off the gangplank and hit the water with an almighty splash. The box was now swinging backwards and forwards over the gap between the ships and, as its linen shroud began to slip, Doris could see that it wasn't a box at all, but a bamboo cage.

Inside it was Cassius of Cyprus.

He noticed Doris immediately.

'Hail, Doris!' he called.

'Hail!' Doris barked back. 'Are you alone? Where are your friends?'

'Gone to Rome,' Cassius replied.

Relieved to hear this, Doris trotted closer to the cage.

She was stopped by one of the ship's officers.

'Take care, Doris,' he said. ''Tis a lion.'

Doris was whisked away to her salon and didn't see Cassius again until an hour or so later, when Charmion came to collect her and take her to the gardens on the upper deck. Caesar and Cleopatra were already there, lounging on couches, and Cassius was sitting beside them.

Doris had been pleased to see the lion arrive safely on board. It was always good to have a fresh face around, even if it was a cat's. Before she'd first met Cassius, at Cleopatra's party, she'd only ever seen marble lions. Now she was faced with the real thing again and, especially without the protection of the cage, she was reminded just how huge and powerful a lion was. Cassius was also wearing a band of gold around his neck. Doris hadn't noticed this when he'd been in the cage, but it, and its matching chain, seemed to make him look more scary than ever.

Cleopatra smiled and patted the seat of her couch.

'Hither, Doris,' she said. 'Come, darling. Sit beside me. You recall Cassius?'

'Of course she does!' Caesar laughed.

Cleopatra tugged on the lion's chain.

'I have bestowed a little gift upon him,' she said. 'What do you think of it, Doris? Do you see how sweetly the gold shines against his fur?'

Doris could see very clearly how sweetly the gold shone against his fur, and wondered why *she* hadn't been bestowed a little gift, too.

She shot a withering look at her mistress and jumped defiantly onto Caesar's knee.

'Fear not, dear Doris,' he said as he wrapped his arms around the slightly miffed poodle. 'He is a sweet cat but he shall never match you in your ma's affection.'

'I should hope not,' Doris muttered.

'You must be nice to Cassius, Doris. He is a guest. Why don't you take him on a tour around our little boat?'

the queen suggested. 'Show him the ropes?'

She raised one arm in the air and snapped her fingers.

'Polygnotus!' she called.

'Oh, please, no,' Doris moaned. 'Not Polygnotus.'

Apart from his habit of pinching her, Polygnotus quite simply gave Doris the creeps. At home in Alexandria she'd always done her best to avoid him, and with some success, since he didn't seem to like her very much either. But here on The State Barge there was no getting away from him. He was like an omnipresent spectre, always lurking, always poised and ready to fawn over the queen and Caesar. So it didn't surprise Doris that hardly had Cleopatra finished calling his name than Polygnotus appeared, apparently from nowhere. He strutted over, bowed ridiculously low and swept one hand along the ground.

'Ah, Polygnotus,' said Caesar. 'Might I congratulate you on your outfit? It is most fetching. I particularly like the colour. Bile green suits you so very well.'

He turned to Cleopatra.

'Don't you think so, darling?' he added.

Cleopatra nodded and clapped a hand over her mouth to suppress a giggle.

'Polygnotus,' Caesar continued as he tried to keep a straight face, 'this is my lion, Cassius.'

Polygnotus bowed again.

'Adorable,' he grovelled.

He reached out to ruffle the top of Cassius's mane,

but something in the lion's eyes made him stop short.

'Please take him and Doris for a walk around the decks,' said Cleopatra.

'My pleasure, Your Exaltedness,' replied Polygnotus slimily.

He took the end of Cassius's chain and the lion got resignedly to his feet and began to follow him. Doris would have preferred to stay where she was, on Caesar's knee, but when Cleopatra gave her a sharp sideways look she knew it wasn't an option. She slumped to the floor and began to pad along behind Cassius, noticing as she did so that Cleopatra had turned to whisper in Caesar's ear.

'You shouldn't tease Polygnotus so,' the queen said.

'Why ever not?' Caesar asked. 'I can't abide the man.'

Doris glanced at Polygnotus to see if he'd heard this remark, but the eunuch's heavily rouged cheeks, dyed lips and emerald green eyelids gave nothing away.

'Ghastly creature,' said Doris to no one in particular.

'Isn't he just!' Cassius growled.

'Caesar can't abide him,' Doris added.

'So I gather,' Cassius replied. 'Has he worked for your mistress very long?'

'I don't really know. Certainly for as long as I've been around. Why do you ask?'

'He seems familiar, that's all.'

'He's a eunuch,' Doris said.

'Yes,' said Cassius. 'I think that's fairly evident.'

'I mean perhaps you're confusing him with another

eunuch. There are lots of them about.'

'No,' Cassius responded. 'I don't think I am.'

Those walks around the deck with Polygnotus became a twice-daily routine for Doris and the lion, and the two animals soon became inseparable friends. The exercise did them good, since the rest of the time all they did was eat and laze about in the sun, but it didn't make either of them like Polygnotus any better. Quite the opposite, in fact.

When Doris told Cassius that Polygnotus sometimes pinched her when no one was looking, the lion said she must tell him next time. He'd make sure it never happened again. He was still convinced he'd seen Polygnotus before, and was infuriated that he couldn't remember where. Doris suggested it might have been at Cleopatra's party, but Cassius said no, it wasn't.

'It was before that,' he insisted. 'I'm sure it was before that.'

CHAPTER TEN
A few days later

Caesar and Cleopatra spent their afternoons dozing on the so-called Private Deck, which was never that private since they were perpetually surrounded by servants and guards. Sometimes this meant as many as thirty people, all of whom had some special task to perform, be it fan-waving, incense-wafting, instrument-playing or chorus-singing. Charmion and Menander were almost always there too, ready to help the queen with her hair and clothes, and Polygnotus was forever nearby, skulking in the shadows.

Cassius and Doris preferred to lie on the bows, where the breeze was cooler, there was no incense to make them sneeze, and Doris could spot crocodiles in peace. They spoke to each other in Felcanish, but they were also teaching each other their respective human languages, Greek and Latin.

Towards the end of one of these lazy afternoons, Cassius caught sight of Menander making his way towards the Private Deck. He was carrying a golden tray laden with pots and bottles, and had a papyrus scroll tucked under one arm.

'I'm bored,' Cassius yawned. 'Let's go and watch whatever Menander's about to do.'

He got up and shook himself.

'Race you!' he growled as he took off at a gallop.

When Menander reached Caesar and Cleopatra, he greeted them with a gracious bow, crossed his ankles and lowered himself to the floor in one fluid movement. He then set down his tray, unrolled his papyrus scroll and spread it over his knee.

'Burnt domestic mice, one part,' he read aloud as Doris and Cassius settled beside him.

He pulled the tray closer, selected a jade bottle with a silver stopper, and held it up.

'Here it is. Also, charred vine-rag,' he added, raising a different bottle. 'Then there's ground horses' teeth, bear's grease, deer's marrow and reed bark; one part of each,' he continued.

'May I?' Cleopatra asked as she leant forward and reached for the jade bottle.

'Of course,' Menander replied.

Cleopatra unscrewed the bottle's stopper, held it to her nose, and sniffed.

'Phew!' she exclaimed, fanning herself with one hand.

'Yuk,' Doris agreed. 'Singed fur and whiskers. What is it?'

'Burnt mice,' said Cassius. '*Very* burnt mice.'

'Well I'm sure it has important properties,' said Doris.

'Menander knows about these things.'

Cleopatra stoppered the bottle and returned it to Menander's tray.

'And thereafter?' she asked.

'I pound the dry ingredients together until I have a fine flour. Then I melt the bear's grease and deer's marrow over a low heat. Next, I mix everything together and add honey to make a paste. This keeps well in a horn cup...'

He held up a horn cup.

'Such as this one. It contains a batch I made earlier. It should be rubbed on Caesar's bald parts until they sprout.'

'Don't tell me he's going to put that on his *head*,' Cassius spluttered.

'Of course he is,' said Doris. 'Menander makes magic potions for all *sorts* of ailments. This one is for baldness.'

'How many applications would you recommend?' Cleopatra inquired.

'Twice daily for one waning of the moon,' Menander replied. 'Thereafter as required.'

'Come then, Caesar,' said Cleopatra.

She took a linen bib from Menander's tray and tied it around Caesar's neck.

Caesar sighed.

'Baldness is a haunting spectre,' he said wistfully. 'And speaking of spectres,' he added, raising his voice, 'is there something you wish to say, Polygnotus?'

The slimy eunuch had been hovering close by, as

usual. Now he stepped forward and made one of his absurd bows.

'Great Caesar,' he cawed. 'I am come to take Doris and Cassius for their afternoon walk.'

'Off you go, then,' said Caesar.

'Might I just point out that I have hair-enhancing recipes of my own?'

'No!' snapped Cleopatra. 'That is Menander's department, and his alone.'

'Walk!' Caesar boomed.

Polygnotus's twice-daily walk had always taken Doris and Cassius on the same route around the barge, although he had occasionally rung the changes by going in the opposite direction. On that day, though, he appeared to be in an adventurous mood. He ignored the usual, well-trodden path which began and ended at the bows of the ship, and made straight for the stern instead.

At first Doris and Cassius thought there'd been some mistake, and so they hovered expectantly and waited for Polygnotus to return. When he didn't, and they heard him calling their names, they looked at each other quizzically and then followed him to the rear of the barge. There they found him standing at the top of a servants' staircase.

'Follow me,' he hissed.

Cassius and Doris looked down. The staircase was steep and narrow, with open treads.

'Have you ever gone down this before?' Cassius asked.

'No,' said Doris. 'But I think it goes to the lower

decks.'

'Why's he taking us there?' Cassius wondered aloud.

'I don't know,' said Doris, trying to sound chirpy. 'Maybe it's a short-cut to my salon?'

'Unlikely. You sleep below the foredeck, next to Cleopatra. We're at the other end of the ship at the moment.'

'I know,' replied Doris in a worried voice.

The further Polygnotus went, the more uneasy Doris felt. He was leading her and Cassius deep into the belly of the ship, to places Doris had never been, nor wished to go.

Here the corridors were narrow and hot and there was only the flicker of an occasional, oxygen-starved lantern to light the way. It was noisy, too, and Doris suddenly realised that the clunking and grinding she could hear was the sound of the oars. She liked to listen to them up on deck, where their rhythm was soothing and they made gentle swishing noises in the water. Down here, though, they sounded like the manpowered machinery they were. Doris wondered just how far she was from the rowers themselves. She knew there were hundreds of them, somewhere. They were pushing and pulling in steaming heat and pitch darkness. Doris was hoping she wasn't going to see them for real when Polygnotus suddenly stopped, looked nervously about him, and pushed open a door.

'Inside!' he whispered hoarsely.

They entered a cabin.

It was furnished with a hammock, a wooden chest and a chair. It was a tiny space, yet it glittered like a jewel shop.

Every surface, even the ceiling, was draped with coloured shawls, tops, skirts and dresses in shades of pink and blue, lilac and lemon. Bangles and necklaces of glass, metal and semi-precious stones were threaded onto ribbons and strung from wall to wall, and the floor was strewn with spangled slippers. On top of the wooden chest was an assortment of bottles and bowls, a tray of combs and hairpins, and a large, ivory box with a silver key. Beside this lay one of Doris's collars. It had a broken buckle which Cleopatra had asked Menander to mend.

Polygnotus sidled up to the ivory box, unlocked it with its silver key, and opened its lid. He moved some of its contents aside, then quickly withdrew something from his sleeve, placed it in the box and covered it up. He'd just closed the lid again when someone walked past the cabin. He turned and froze, then waited for several seconds before tiptoeing across the room and slowly opening the door.

'You first,' he said as he shoved Cassius ahead of him.

When there were no screams of alarm, Polygnotus scooped Doris up in his spidery hands and followed Cassius back along the corridors and up the steps until they reached the top deck.

Doris blinked in the bright sunshine.

'That was Menander's cabin,' she told Cassius. 'I

recognised some of his clothes and one of my collars.'

'Then Menander is going to be in a great deal of trouble very soon,' Cassius replied.

'Because of what Polygnotus put there?' asked Doris.

Cassius nodded.

'What do you think it was?'

'I've no idea, but it won't be good.'

'Why do you think he took us with him?'

'In case someone saw him,' Cassius supposed. 'His own cabin is on the port side. Menander's cabin is starboard, and Polygnotus has no business on that part of the ship. He'd have had trouble explaining himself if he'd been caught. With us there he could always pretend that we'd run off and he'd chased after us. The real question is what did he put in the box?'

'Do you think we can we get it back again?'

'We must,' Cassius replied as a horn sounded. 'But later. We can't go missing now. It's dinner time. They'll only wonder why we haven't appeared and send someone to look for us. That could make things worse, especially if they found us just as we unearthed Polygnotus's secret. They'd think it belonged to Menander, which is probably the whole idea.'

When Doris and Cassius reached the Private Deck, Caesar and Cleopatra were still there with Menander standing behind them, scraping the bottom of his horn jar with a spatula. The top of Caesar's head was already covered in green sludge, but Menander was determined to winkle out and use every last grain of his special potion.

'Hail, Doris, Cassius!' Caesar called, ignoring Polygnotus. 'Enjoy your walk? Come, sit with us. It's time to eat.'

Handmaidens arrived to lay the table and set down jars of water and wine, and Caesar agreed, somewhat reluctantly, to keep the hair restorative on his head until dinner was over. Menander then left, taking his papyrus and his tray of bottles and jars with him, and saying he would return later to shampoo Caesar's hair and massage his scalp with some special oils.

The food on The State Barge was much simpler than that at the palace in Alexandria. Caesar didn't have a huge appetite and often ate nothing but fruit during the day. Even at dinner, he wasn't particularly interested in fancy dishes. He was by nature a lover of routine, and liked his food to be served plain, punctually and at predetermined times.

This made a refreshing change for the queen's chef, Demetrius. He didn't have to repeatedly cook flamboyant meals until Cleopatra deigned to send for them. Instead, he could spend his time finding ingredients which Caesar would enjoy for their freshness and flavour. The Nile was teeming with delicious fish, and many herbs and vegetables were grown along her lush green banks, so every morning Demetrius would leave the barge by rowing boat and go on a shopping expedition. There he would hand-pick produce at one of the many mud brick villages which lined the shore, and try to find something special for Caesar.

That evening, Demetrius arrived on deck looking particularly pleased with himself. He was carrying a steaming platter of succulent pink meat, and was beaming from ear to ear.

'And this is?' Cleopatra enquired.

'Liver of hippopotamus,' the chef replied with a blush.

The queen clapped her hands in delight.

'*Marvellous*!' she said.

'One of your favourites,' Demetrius smiled affectionately.

He had cooked for Cleopatra all her life and knew every nuance of her likes and dislikes.

'You're right!' Cleopatra giggled. 'I *love* liver of hippopotamus!'

She turned to Caesar.

'You must try this,' she told him, 'for it is a rare treat and full of goodness.'

Caesar wrinkled his nose.

'Come now,' Cleopatra laughed. 'He who hesitates is lost.'

Caesar grudgingly delved into the folds of his toga and removed his personal golden eating knife whilst Cleopatra continued to expound the virtues of hippopotamus liver.

'...but the beasts themselves are *very* dangerous,' she added, 'and cause many an untimely death.'

Caesar leant forward and speared a portion of the meat with his knife.

'They appear harmless,' Cleopatra went on. 'They all look much the same, of course. But that is the very heart of the problem. It is difficult to tell one from the other. Yet some are possessive and spiteful...'

''Sounds like a certain eunuch I know,' Doris mumbled.

Caesar raised the knife to his mouth.

'They can be secret killers and...'

Cassius tensed.

'What? What's wrong, Cassius?' Doris asked.

'That's *it*!' the lion roared.

'*What*? What's *what*?'

'The knife! Get the knife!'

Cassius leapt into the air and Doris saw his black mane float, as if in slow motion. She followed his lead, springing upwards until she felt her head collide with his. She heard a squeal from Cleopatra and a gasp from Caesar, and the knife sprang from Caesar's hand, hit the deck with a 'ping', and skittered across the boards.

In the commotion that followed, Doris took the chance to return to Menander's cabin. She ran to the ship's stern and hurtled back down the narrow steps to the lower decks. The scent of Cassius still lingered in the darkened corridors and she used it to guide her as she raced through the servants' quarters. She reached Menander's cabin and barked, but she didn't wait for him to open the door. Instead, she flung herself hard against it, making contact just as Menander opened it from the inside. That took her unawares, and she was catapulted through the doorway and landed in a heap on the cabin floor.

'Oh, my *darling*!' Menander half laughed. 'Are you all right?'

She was.

She struggled quickly to her feet, spun round, and located the box with the silver key. She swiped at it with her paw and knocked it sideways. It clattered to the floor, and its lid, which Polygnotus had closed but not locked, fell open.

'Doris? What are you...?'

She scrabbled furiously through the contents of the box. She didn't know what she was looking for, but she dismissed anything which smelled of herself, Menander or Cleopatra. She dug down deep with her paws, tossing things aside until she found an alabaster phial.

Menander was laughing properly by now. He tried to pick her up but she wriggled free, caught the phial between her teeth and ran through the cabin door.

'Ah! I see!' Menander called after her. 'You want me to chase you! I'll count to ten, and then *I'm coming to get you*! One...'

Doris closed her mouth against the phial. Its surface was slippery but she managed to hold on until she reached the upper deck.

Once there, she opened her jaws and the phial dropped onto the deck and rolled overboard, into the Nile.

Seconds later, Cassius arrived at her side.

'What have you *done?*' he asked.

'I...'

Doris was seeing double. Her mouth was dry and she was terribly, terribly thirsty.

'Cassius, I...'

She stumbled against the lion's side. Her legs buckled beneath her and her head began to fizz. Something nudged her. She felt a set of teeth close around the scruff of her neck and then everything went black.

CHAPTER ELEVEN
A few days later

Over the next few days and nights, Doris slipped in and out of consciousness.

She was only vaguely aware of the goings-on around her but Menander never left her side, and Caesar and Cleopatra came to visit her often. They mopped her brow with cooling poultices, held her hot paws in their hands and sponged her clammy fur. She was still desperately thirsty, but sometimes the liquid she gulped down wasn't water but castor oil, which made her vomit horribly. When that happened, Menander would stroke her, apologise profusely, and tell her that it was all part of the cure, and therefore must be done.

She shivered a lot, and felt hot and cold all at once. Her eyes couldn't tell the difference between dark and light and, when she managed to sleep, she had terrible nightmares about Polygnotus. She'd wake up howling, and Menander would send for Cassius and Cleopatra, if they weren't already there. Then the lion would lie down beside his poodle friend and wrap his big, warm paws around her whilst her mistress sang a soothing lullaby.

Long before she was strong enough to walk again, but after the worst of her symptoms had passed, Cassius told Doris what had happened.

'Cleopatra was talking about hippos. She said they could be possessive and spiteful, and you said something about that reminding you of Polygnotus. Cleopatra then went on to say that some hippos were killers. That made me think. We knew that Polygnotus had hidden something in Menander's cabin. Could that something be poison? Was Polygnotus a killer? I didn't analyse it any more than that, I didn't have time. I thought the poison was probably in the meat...'

'No. It couldn't have been. Demetrius would never let that happen...'

Cassius raised a paw.

'I didn't know that,' he said. 'All I knew was that Caesar had some of the meat on his knife, so I just leapt for it. There was total confusion after that. Caesar even whacked me over the head for frightening your mistress.'

'Ooh. Did that *hurt?*'

'Hardly. It was only a cuff. Then I noticed you were missing. I realised you'd gone back to Menander's cabin to recover whatever Polygnotus had hidden there. Supposing it was a stash of poison? I ran to the stern and found you. I knew straightaway that you'd been poisoned. I picked you up by the scruff of your neck and carried you back to your mistress. Menander had appeared by then, but he didn't try to take you away from me. He knew I could get you to Cleopatra faster than he could. You were limp as a rag, Doris. You were dying. Cleopatra was beside herself. She sent for her toxicologist...'

'I know him,' Doris interrupted. 'He's my ma's poison expert. He's travelling on one of the escort ships. He sometimes tastes her food for her, but only at a stranger's house. He hardly ever tastes something Demetrius has cooked. Demetrius would rather *die* than let poison into his kitchens.'

'Well anyway, the toxicologist arrived, took one look at you, and turned completely grey. He didn't need to ask what the problem was. He could see how poorly you were, but he said he couldn't prescribe an antidote until he knew what had happened before you fell ill. It was then he was told about Caesar's eating knife. No one had touched it. I think they were still reeling from my behaviour. The toxicologist pulled on a pair of cotton gloves, picked up the knife and tipped it backwards and forwards against the light. "This is not Caesar's knife,' he said. "It is a copy, and a skillful one, at that."

'No!'

Cassius nodded.

'He showed us a very fine slit along the knife's top edge and explained that it was the opening to a hollow cavity. Then he brushed the blade with his index finger and held the finger up. "Atropos," he said. He was very glum. Your mistress gasped and shot a hand to her mouth.'

'What's atropos?' Doris asked.

'A plant. Also known as "That which cuts the thread

of life." The toxicologist confirmed your symptoms. He said you had atropos poisoning. He decided you must have mouthed the knife when we leapt at it.'

'But I didn't,' Doris protested. 'I didn't get anywhere near it!'

'I know. What did you find in Menander's cabin, Doris?'

'A phial. I carried it back to the starboard deck, but then I dropped it and it fell overboard.'

'You didn't touch the knife. Neither of us did. That proves the phial contained atropos,' Cassius purred. 'There must have been traces of it on its surface.'

'It *did* feel slippery,' Doris remembered, 'But why did Polygnotus hide it in Menander's cabin? Why not throw it overboard himself?

'In case something went wrong and he needed a second shot at Caesar, I suppose. He wanted to keep the phial but he also knew that if things went *really* wrong...'

'As they did...'

'...then the queen would order a search of the barge. Polygnotus certainly wouldn't want the phial to be found in *his* quarters. He could have hidden it anywhere, but he deliberately chose Menander's cabin. He wanted Menander to be blamed for the poisoning because he's jealous of him.'

'I don't think Cleopatra would have fallen for that,' said Doris. 'She'd never have believed Menander was the poisoner.'

'That would have been irrelevant. She would have

had to have Menander executed, whatever she believed. People in her position can't be seen to have favourites. It shows a weakness, like a chink in their armour. Thankfully it never came to that.'

'Did they search the barge?'

'Yes. They didn't find anything, of course.'

'Because I'd already found it,' Doris sighed.

'Was Menander in his cabin?'

'Yes.'

'He didn't tell anybody, thank goodness. He never said you'd been there, never mentioned what you'd found.'

'He didn't know. He didn't see what was in my mouth. He just thought I was playing, trying to get him to chase me. I often do that.'

'He doesn't know you saved his life.'

'I don't mind about that,' Doris answered. 'I just want to know who put the poison in the knife. Was it Polygnotus?'

'Who else? He must have laced the fake knife with atropos then swapped it with for the real one. That was the easy part. You've seen the way he hovers over Caesar and the queen whilst they sleep in the sun. He's always adjusting their clothes and plumping up their cushions.'

'But how was the knife copied in the first place? Caesar hardly lets it out of his sight.'

'That's the bit I can't work out,' said Cassius. 'And it worries me. I think Polygnotus must have...'

Cassius groaned, lay down heavily and folded his paws over his head.

'Oh, but of course!' he said. 'That's it! Lux et veritas!'

'The truth will out? *What* truth, Cassius?' Doris yelped. 'What have you thought of?'

'Polygnotus,' the lion replied. 'I *knew* I'd seen him somewhere before. Now I've remembered where. And when. It was long before I met *you*. It was probably before you were even born. I was in Rome, and one of Caesar's centurions was taking me for a walk. A eunuch came sidling up and started asking all sorts of questions about me. Where I'd come from, how old I was, things like that.'

'The sort of things anyone might ask.'

'Yes. But nobody ever did, you see. I wasn't a pretty little poodle like you. I was a lion, Caesar's lion, and there was a centurion on the end of my lead. You don't go quizzing centurions, with or without lions. They're hardened soldiers and they don't take kindly to being quizzed. Most people give centurions a wide berth, but not this man. That's why I remember it. But it hardly matters now.'

'Except that it proves that Polygnotus was in Rome, so presumably he met people there and kept in touch with them after he came to Egypt,' said Doris.

Cassius nodded.

'We don't know when that was,' he said, 'but at some point he took employment with your mistress.'

'He's been around for as long as *I* can remember. He must have come here shortly after you met him. Before I was born, before the queen went into exile.'

'He couldn't have known then that Caesar would come to Egypt. And yet he kept in touch with his contacts in Rome...'

'What are you saying, Cassius?'

The lion laid a paw on Doris's back.

'*I* don't know. I think Polygnotus probably came here to spy on Cleopatra. He must have been livid that he couldn't get close to her, but then he got lucky. Or at least he thought he did. Suddenly, from out of nowhere, he had an opportunity to poison Caesar. He got back in touch with his mates in Rome, named his price and waited for instructions. Then someone came up with the knife idea. It was they who ordered the fake, but it must have passed through many hands before it got here. Polygnotus would have been the last link in a very long chain.'

'So all Polygnotus had to do was buy the...what's it called?'

'Atropos.'

'...atropos and put it in the blade.'

'It's easy to buy, apparently. The toxicologist said it's used in medicines. In greatly diluted quantities of course, otherwise it's lethal. If Polygnotus had succeeded and Caesar had died, Polygnotus would have been paid a fortune. Either that, or he'd have had his throat slit to keep him quiet. Which may yet happen.'

'What do you think he'll do now?' Doris asked.

'It'll be interesting to see. I doubt he realises you found the phial. Why would he? He thinks you were poisoned by the knife. He probably thinks the searchers missed the phial and it's still Menander's cabin. He'll go back there to try to recover it...'

'And realise it's already is gone...'

'Yes.'

'Then what?'

'He'll panic, I suppose. Who knows? Who cares?'

By the time the Royal Barge reached Heliopolis, Doris was feeling much better and was allowed to leave her sick bay. On her first evening out, she lay in Cleopatra's arms and watched the sun go down on the Sphinx and the three great pyramids at El Giza.

'They are truly Egyptian,' Cleopatra said wistfully, 'and very ancient. They have stood here for more than two-thousand years. See how they glow? They are surfaced with polished white limestone. So beautiful.'

She began to weep, and Caesar wrapped an arm around her and pulled her close to him.

'To think you might never have seen them,' the queen sobbed. 'Had it not been for Doris and Cassius. Had they not knocked that knife from your hands...'

'Sshht, now. Let's not dwell on what *might* have happened,' Caesar soothed.

He patted Cassius's mane and stroked Doris's back.

'Let's just be grateful for our wonderful pets, and what they did for us,' he added.

Caesar and Cleopatra thought the murder plot had probably originated in Rome. As to the swapping of the knives, that could have happened anywhere, but it seemed likely it was done on the barge.

The one thing that was known for certain was that the poison could *only* have been applied on the barge, and *only* in the hours between midmorning, when Caesar had used the knife to cut some fruit, and the evening itself.

Cleopatra had been willing to have everyone who might have had access to Caesar's knife put to death. The executions would have numbered scores and included Menander and Charmion because, as Cassius had pointed out, great leaders could not be seen to have favourites. Caesar had vetoed that idea. He would not have been any the wiser, and Cleopatra would have lost some of her most trusted servants for nothing.

'We have our suspicions,' Caesar had said. 'Veritatem dies aperit. Time reveals the truth.'

'We shall leave Sebek to make his judgement,' Cleopatra had vowed. 'Sebek will be the judge.'

Sebek was the Egyptian god who overcame difficulties and repaired evil doings.

Like all gods, he had an earthly guise.

Sebek was a crocodile.

At Aswan, The State Barge turned in the water to head home. Doris was snoozing on the bows at the time, and was woken by a sudden commotion. She raised her head from her paws and saw Cassius bounding towards her.

'Man overboard!' the lion roared. 'Quick, quick, Doris! Come and see!'

Doris leapt to her feet.

'Whereabouts?' she asked excitedly.

'On the port side, towards the stern,' Cassius replied. 'There's quite a to-do, I can tell you.'

As the two friends rushed along the barge, they were joined by ship's officers, handmaidens and servants who had heard the news, or at least the noise, and had dropped what they were doing to hurry to its source. Doris and Cassius galloped ahead, and were soon about two-thirds along the ship's port rails.

They stopped and looked down.

The first thing they noticed was that, although the oars had been lifted clear of the water and the ship was hardly moving, the river was absolutely churning. Her normally placid blue waters had whipped into an angry brown froth of strange crosscurrents and sudden swells.

'Why's it doing that?' Doris asked.

'Crocs,' said Cassius calmly.

Doris took a step back.

'*What*?'

'Crocs,' the lion said again.

'But what about the man? The man in the water!' Doris squealed. 'Someone should get him out of there!'

'Oh? Are you volunteering?'

'Hold on to me,' said Doris.

She wriggled under Cassius's chest, squeezed herself between his forelegs, and pressed her nose against the railings.

She could see the crocodiles more clearly now. There were four or more of them thrashing about in the water. They had torn something apart and were now competing for it, ripping it to pieces and spinning their whole bodies in a frenzied effort to snap its last remaining threads.

Doris watched in awe as shreds of flotsam rose to the surface and bobbed on the waves.

They were almost pretty.

Little bits of pink and blue, lilac and lemon and palest green.

'*NO!*' she howled. 'Get him *out*, Cassius! Get him out of the *water*!'

'Hush, Doris,' Cassius soothed. 'It's not Menander. Look. He's over there.'

Doris turned and saw with relief that Cassius was right. Menander was standing close by, safe and dry.

'Then who?' she asked. 'Who is it? Is it...?'

'Yes and no,' said Cassius. 'Look again, Doris. What do you see?'

Doris peered at the churning waters.

'Crocs,' she said. 'And bits of coloured cloth.'

'Any blood?'

'No. How peculiar. There's no blood.'

'Not peculiar at all. I think Polygnotus threw something overboard to distract Sebek and his friends. That something was already dead, and dead bodies don't bleed. Polygnotus wrapped it up in a few of his frocks to make it look like him, waited for it to get the crocs' attention, then jumped off the other side of the ship.'

'Well either way, he's gone,' sighed Doris.

'Gone but not forgotten,' said Cassius. 'And probably not dead either.'

'Oh. What a shame.'

'No shame, Doris. I relish the chance that he's still

alive. Yum, yum,' the lion smacked his lips, 'traitors are my favourite snack.'

There was another commotion later that day, when Demetrius discovered that the main ingredient for that night's dinner had gone missing.

'How can a whole side of antelope just disappear?' he wailed. 'I've been hanging that meat for *weeks*! It was perfect.'

Cassius turned to Doris and winked.

'Told you,' he said.

CHAPTER TWELVE
Bo's House.
The 21st Century

'Thanks for the warning,' Bo huffed when she got back to her own time.

'About what?' Cavendish asked.

'About Doris being poisoned for a start,' Bo said. 'She could have died.'

'She could, but she didn't,' the spaniel pointed out. 'Subtle difference.'

'Very subtle,' Bo snorted. 'Which is not something you can say about albatross, or whatever it's called. It's lethal, apparently.'

'Atropos. Otherwise known as Deadly Nightshade,' came the curt reply.

Bo looked sideways at her friend. His normally friendly face was distinctly stony.

'What's the matter?' she asked.

'You know Bo, you don't have to do any of this,' Cavendish growled. 'You can stay here and be boring. And frankly I'd rather you did if you're going to blame me every time something doesn't go your way. Doris's life wasn't all about fancy parties. She had to take the rough with the smooth, and so should you.'

'Sorry,' Bo apologized. 'But it's hard sometimes. You forget that I don't know what you know, or even how you *know* it.'

'Then ask me a question. Any question.'

'All right,' Bo replied. 'How did you know about the Nile cruise?'

'That's easy. It's well-documented.'

Bo huffed.

'Then how did you know that Polygnotus would jump in with the crocodiles?'

'I didn't. You said he was a reptile and I said he'd soon be among friends. I didn't think he'd actually go swimming with them.'

Bo racked her brains for another question.

'How about this, then? Cassius told Doris that when the cruise ended, he and Caesar would probably have to leave Egypt and go back to Rome...'

'And your question is?'

'Did they?'

'Yes.'

'So did Doris see them again?'

'Didn't Cassius also once say that all roads lead to Rome?' asked Cavendish.

'Yes,' said Bo. 'He did.'

'Well, then. There's your answer.'

CHAPTER THIRTEEN
Rome, Italy.
14th March 44 BC

Doris had been in Rome for eighteen months.

She and Cleopatra had borrowed a beautiful villa. It belonged to Caesar and was nestled in its own private estate at the foot of the Janiculum Hill, just across the Tiber River from the city itself.

When the morning mists cleared, Doris would sit on the dewy lawn and look across the river to the roofs of Rome and the seven hills beyond. The river was narrow, compared to the Nile. Its waters had a yellow tinge and it had no splendid boats like the dhows of Egypt, but it did have barges, and Doris loved to listen to the familiar rhythm of their oars swishing through the water.

It reminded her of home.

She missed the gentle sea breezes of Alexandria, but there was compensation in the villa's shady gardens. They had trees and shrubs that Doris had never seen before and, when the sun became too hot, she would retreat into their lush greenness. Sometimes, deer strayed into them, too, and there were always hares to chase. These timid creatures were easily seen off, but if Doris ran into a wild boar she'd have to bark until a gardener came to rescue her. The man would wave his arms and shout, and the boar would stare back and kick up the soil with its trotters, then turn and hurtle away.

When the air cooled, Doris would leave the lawns and head for the terraces. These formal gardens were very similar to those at the palace in Alexandria, with statues, colonnades and borders defined by miniature hedges.

There were even gardens inside the villa, painted onto the walls. Some of these had frames around them, as if they were being seen through a window. There were fences in the foreground, mountains in the distance, and flowers and darting birds in the middle. Doris could spend hours staring at these paintings, but her favourite game was looking at the villa's mosaic floors. These were made from thousands of tiny squares of different coloured stone. When Doris was standing on top of them, they seemed like a meaningless jumble, but as soon as she jumped on a couch and looked down, she could see that they were beautiful pictures. Her favourite was of a dolphin leaping through waves.

Doris was happy in Rome. She had the gardens, Caesar and Cassius were living nearby, and she had Cleopatra. And since Cleopatra had brought most of her considerable entourage, including Doris's favourites, Menander, Charmion and Demetrius, it was almost like home. If Doris had one complaint, it was that it was hard to get any peace in the evenings. Cleopatra was more sociable than ever, there was a steady stream of visitors and, because the villa was so much smaller than the palace at Alexandria, it was difficult for Doris to escape.

The evening of 14th March was unusually intimate.

Cleopatra had no guests, and she and Doris were lazing on the villa's verandah and watching the sun go down. Sitting between them was Cleopatra's baby boy, Caesarion, who was the son of Julius Caesar.

Doris lapped her spring water with its garnish of floating violet petals and considered her next move.

'Shall I have a stroll around the gardens? It's such a lovely evening. Or perhaps a nap before dinner?'

She'd just plumped for the stroll when Cleopatra rang a little golden bell.

A nursemaid scuttled forward and Cleopatra kissed Caesarion good night and handed him over.

'It is time for his bed,' she told the nurse. 'And I am ready for Menander. Tell him to come to me. Quickly, please.'

'Mmm. Menander,' Doris pondered. 'I think I might not walk, after all. I might just stay here instead.'

Minutes later, Menander arrived to brush out the queen's hair, something he did every evening.

He set down his trusty tray of brushes and combs, pins, jewelled ornaments and hair-slides, and Doris snuggled up against her mistress to watch the proceedings. Having her hair brushed was one of Cleopatra's favourite rituals and a rare opportunity for her to relax. Doris knew how she felt. It was one of *her* favourite rituals, too, but her

101

mistress seemed unusually twitchy that night. Rather than insisting on her customary one-hundred strokes of the brush, Cleopatra held up her hand after only twenty-two.

'That will do very well,' she said brusquely.

Almost without looking, she selected a pair of ivory and lapis combs and picked them up from the tray.

'Put them in swiftly, Menander,' she added as she passed them over her shoulder. 'And do it well, for Caesar is but moments away.'

Doris sat bolt upright.

'Caesar but *moments* away?' she yelped. 'Then I must run to the gate and meet him!'

She leapt off the couch and bounded down the verandah's steps.

'Doris!' Cleopatra shouted after her. 'Come back this instant! You must have your hair dressed for Caesar's delight.'

'Not tonight, ma,' Doris barked back as she charged through the gardens. 'Tonight I shall delight him with... with...something else! Something like...'

Her eyes darted to and fro until she spotted a rosemary bush. She skidded to a halt beside it, selected a perfect sprig and snapped its stalk with her teeth.

'...this rosemary!'

When Caesar arrived at the villa's gates, Doris sprang through the open side of his litter and settled herself on his lap.

'Ha! Doris!' he exclaimed, wrapping his arms around

her. 'What's this? A sprig of rosemary?'

He took Doris's gift and held it against his chest.

'I shall keep it here,' he said, 'next to my heart. Rosemary is a sacred plant, you know. It is said to aid the concentration. Which makes it most pertinent this night, for Cleopatra and I have much to discuss and an important decision to make.'

He ruffled the fur on Doris's head.

'Well-chosen, Doris,' he laughed. 'Now then. Take me to your mistress.'

Back on the verandah, Doris lay on Caesar's couch whilst he ate his dinner. When he'd finished, he asked the servants to bring more wine, a shawl for Cleopatra, and some extra lanterns. Then he ordered them to close the shutters on every window that overlooked the verandah, and dismissed them for the night.

'Except for Menander,' Cleopatra interjected. 'Ask Menander to wait up. Tell him I will ring the bell when I need him.'

When the servants had gone, Caesar began to talk in a voice so low that Doris had to strain to hear what he was saying. He mentioned his achievements, the power he held, and the extraordinary growth of Rome, whose lands now reached further than ever.

'That is all thanks to you, my darling,' Cleopatra whispered. 'And you haven't finished yet.'

'No,' said Caesar. 'There is still Parthia.'

Doris trembled.

She'd heard about Parthia.

It was a vast, mysterious and fabulously wealthy land which had never been defeated. Some said it never could be. But it was also the gateway to the east and to places like India, where there were riches beyond imagination. Whoever conquered Parthia would dominate the world. Doris would just rather that person wasn't Caesar. She wanted him to stay at home. He was already powerful. He had Cleopatra and her money, their baby son and Doris. What more could anyone want?

Whilst Doris was thinking about Parthia, Caesar and Cleopatra were talking about it.

It seemed that Caesar's plans to invade it had gone further than Doris knew. His army was already prepared but, as Doris shifted on his lap and looked into his face, she could see that, for all his bravado, he was worried.

'I should take heed of the oracles,' he suddenly said.

Doris pricked up her ears. This would be interesting.

The oracles were precious books which were thought to hold the answer to any question asked of them. Even the bravest and most educated Romans were afraid to ignore what the oracles said.

'I asked them what the outcome would be if I invaded Parthia,' Caesar explained. 'But their reply wasn't good. They said I couldn't defeat Parthia without first becoming a king. There is no such thing as a Roman king. Rome hates the very idea of kings. My soldiers hate it, too. But they believe in the oracles. They will refuse to fight Parthia if I am not made a king.'

He fiddled with Doris's ears.

'And so,' he continued, 'I find myself in unfamiliar territory. Julius Caesar in a no-win situation, eh? Who'd have thought it, Doris?'

He pulled Doris onto his knee and took Cleopatra's hands in his. Like that, the three of them sat together in silence and watched the fireflies dancing in the dark. The oracles appeared to have talked Caesar out of Parthia, and Doris was glad. She listened contentedly as Caesar and Cleopatra began to talk about lighter things. They discussed good friends, beautiful gardens and the holidays they wanted to take together. When the night turned chilly and everyone was tired, Cleopatra picked up her little golden bell and rang it three times.

Within seconds, Menander arrived. He was holding Doris's zebra skin blanket and her most sacred and lucky collar, the purple silk of Isis with lapis Iwiw charms.

'That's strange,' Doris mumbled. 'Why's he brought those out now? It's bedtime.'

The answer came from Cleopatra.

'You are to go with Caesar this night,' she explained.

Doris wagged her tail.

'*Yes!*' she barked.

She stood on her hind legs, braced her front paws against Caesar's chest and took a long, cat-like stretch.

Caesar stroked her back and hitched her into his arms and Cleopatra kissed them both good night. She also whispered something to Caesar, and Doris, who was right next to him, heard every word.

'Propose it to the Senate, my love,' the queen urged. 'Ask them to make you king. If they do that, your soldiers will follow you to Parthia and you will achieve your greatest ambition.'

'Or I could settle for my *second* greatest ambition,' Caesar whispered back. 'I could conquer the Britons instead.'

'The *Britons*?' Cleopatra giggled. 'But they are an *island* race! They have no trade or *treasure*! They are but savages. What business could you possibly have with *them*?'

'*Interesting* business,' Caesar replied. 'The Britons *interest* me. I admire their courage. But you're right. They have little to offer in the way of wealth...'

'For that, dear Caesar, you must go to Parthia.'

'Parthia? Oh, yes. Parthia is much the better option.'

'Oh, *no*,' thought Doris despairingly.

Caesar carried Doris to his litter, settled her on her zebra blanket and climbed in beside her.

'I'll bring you back tomorrow, Doris,' he said a little shakily. 'After I am proclaimed king. We shall have a special banquet to celebrate. You will be the guest of honour and Demetrius will prepare all your favourite foods. Won't *that* be exciting!'

Doris did her best to look pleased. She even tried to visualize the cage of dormice which Demetrius was fattening up at the bottom of the garden. But it was no good. She was disappointed and frightened. Caesar hadn't changed his mind at all. He still intended to invade

Parthia. He wrapped his arms around her and patted her gently on her head, and Doris noticed that he, like her, was trembling.

At the gates of his home in the city, Caesar ordered the litter bearers to stop.

'You are dismissed for this night,' he told them. 'Doris and I will walk the rest of the way.'

'Then we must walk with you,' one of the men replied, 'and see Caesar safely home.'

'I *am* home!' Caesar barked. 'Leave us!'

'Until tomorrow, then,' the bearers replied nervously.

But Caesar was already waving them away and walking briskly towards his house.

'It is but a short distance,' he told Doris as she trotted along beside him, 'and I need some air...'

He stopped on the path and cupped a hand over one ear.

'...do you hear something?'

Doris listened.

All she could hear was the noisy singing of cicadas, but there *was* a strong, and very familiar, smell.

She barked, and Caesar laughed.

'Watch,' he chuckled.

He opened his mouth, pressed two fingers against his tongue and made a piercing whistle. There was a whoosh of undergrowth and a rustle of leaves, and Cassius bounded onto the path. He padded to within a pace of Caesar, reared up on his hind legs and flung his front paws around his master's neck.

'Don't do that to me,' muttered Doris.

'See, Doris,' said Caesar as he clapped the big cat's spotted underbelly. ''Tis only your lion friend. He will take you for a turn around the gardens. And then we must retire to bed.'

The lion thumped back to earth, and Caesar laughed again and continued on his way.

Doris had seen Cassius many times during her stay in Rome but she had never seen him so subdued. He said nothing until Caesar was safely inside the house, then he bent close and spoke in her ear.

'It's good to see you, Doris,' he whispered. 'But I have grim news. They say that Caesar's cavalry horses are weeping and won't eat. Worse, a little bird flew into Pompey's Hall today. It was carrying a sprig of laurel in its beak but it was chased down by other birds and killed. These are bad omens. Do you know old Spurinna, the soothsayer?' the lion enquired.

Doris nodded sagely.

'Yes, yes. Very well indeed,' she lied.

'Spurinna gave Caesar a warning,' Cassius continued. 'She told him beware the ides of March. That's tomorrow, the very day the Senate meets.'

'I think Caesar might ask them to make him king,' said Doris. 'He wants to conquer Parthia, but the oracles say he won't do it unless he's a king.'

Cassius nodded.

'You're right,' he said. 'And that's why you're here.

Caesar intends to take you to the Senate as his lucky talisman. But there are those who think he has too much power already, and Rome has never liked kingship.'

Cassius was clearly very worried.

'What will happen?' asked Doris.

'I don't know,' the lion replied.

'Well it won't be anything bad,' Doris announced with utter conviction. 'The goddess Isis won't let anything *bad* happen.'

'I'm afraid the goddess Isis is part of the problem, Doris. The Romans don't trust Cleopatra. They see her as an eastern queen with strange ways. They don't understand her, and that frightens them.'

'She's not eastern, she's Greek.'

'She's the Greek queen of an eastern country. That's double trouble. The Romans hate the Greeks and always have done. It's jealousy. They copy Greek fashions but then snigger behind their hands and say the Greeks are no better than drunken peasants. Roman society ladies are the worst. They're nothing but two-faced prudes.'

Doris gasped.

'Don't sound so surprised,' Cassius said. 'I come from Africa, remember? What do I care about Romans? My loyalty is to Caesar. It's him I love, not them.'

'Caesar will be fine. Don't worry, Cassius. It'll be all right. So what if he's not made a king? It'll mean he can't go to Parthia. He'll stay home with you and me. That's a good thing, isn't it?'

'Yes,' said Cassius. 'That's a very good thing.'

Looking only slightly happier, Cassius saw Doris

safely to the door of the villa.

'Good night, dear lion,' said Doris.

She stood on her hind legs and patted the top of her friend's mane with her paws. Then she slid her front legs over his ears and settled them on his shoulders.

'Good night,' she added as she kissed his nose.

'Good night,' Cassius replied. 'Sweet dreams.'

Doris found Caesar waiting in the hall.

A woman was standing next to him, holding his hand.

'Ah! Here she is,' Caesar said as Doris trotted up to him. 'Doris? This is my wife, Calpurnia.'

Doris couldn't think why it hadn't occurred to her that Caesar's wife might be here. Everyone knew she existed, including Cleopatra. Still, Doris felt awkward, running into her suddenly like this. Caesar seemed to understand, and picked her up so that she and Calpurnia could meet each other face to face.

'She's nice,' thought Doris as Calpurnia reached out to stroke her ears.

'There,' said Caesar. 'Now let's all go to bed. Big day, tomorrow.'

Doris was fast asleep at the foot of Caesar's bed when something woke her. She sat up on her zebra skin and glanced anxiously around the room. The shutters and doors were firmly closed, all was still and quiet, and Caesar and Calpurnia were sleeping soundly.

Doris sighed and lay down again. She lowered her

head to her paws and began to relax. The moon was shining through the gaps between the shutters' slats and casting silver stripes on the otherwise darkened room. She watched these stripes until her eyelids grew heavy, the stripes and her zebra skin blurred into one, and she dozed off.

In the middle of the night, there was an almighty bang and all three occupants of the bed sat bolt upright, eyes staring. The shutters and doors had slammed wide open. Now they were tapping the walls and creaking in the wind. Black shadows danced on the ceiling and shards of plaster shivered and dropped to the floor.

'It is another bad omen,' Calpurnia whispered in a trembling voice. 'First it was the cavalry horses, then the bird in Pompey's Hall, now this. Do not go to the Senate in the morning, Julius. I beg you. Do not go.'

Caesar put an arm around her shoulder.

'Perhaps you're right,' he said as he patted the bedclothes and Doris tottered towards him. 'I must reconsider.'

Doris snuggled between Caesar and Calpurnia and tried to stop shaking. The three of them sat together in silence for a long time, but eventually Caesar and Calpurnia fell into a fitful sleep. Both were restless, and Doris had to move to avoid being hit by their flailing arms. She clambered back to the foot of the bed but she didn't lie down. She sat staring through the window at the blue moon and the seven hills of Rome. She kept watch all

111

night until the moon faded away and the orange ball of the sun rose in its place.

The ides of March had dawned.

CHAPTER FOURTEEN
Caesar's House, Rome, Italy.
15th March 44 BC

Calpurnia must have known that her husband was having an affair with Cleopatra, and that they had had a son together. She must also have known that Doris was Cleopatra's pet, if only because of the purple collar of Isis, which no other dog would have dared to wear. Yet she was very kind to Doris that morning, and spoke gently to her whilst she fastened the collar and fed her some breakfast.

Meanwhile, Caesar paced up and down, dithered about and finally announced that he'd decided not to go to the meeting of the Senate after all.

No one was more relieved than Doris, but that soon ended when a man named Decimus arrived at the villa. He was an old friend of Caesar's and had come to ask why Caesar was so late for the meeting. When Caesar said he wasn't going, Decimus said that he must.

To Doris's horror, Caesar changed his mind again. He summoned his litter and asked Calpurnia to bring him his papers and stylus. Then he went to his room and quickly reemerged wearing a pristine, freshly laundered

toga. He scooped Doris up, grabbed his papers, his stylus
and his sacred purple cloak, and strode purposefully to
the waiting litter.

The bearers set off at a brisk trot, but they were soon
having to push and jostle their way through the crushed
streets of Rome. This was Doris's first venture into the
heart of the city, and she'd never seen anything like it.
She pressed her nose against the litter's side and gawked
in amazement. She saw shackled slaves, fine ladies, big
soldiers, small children and many mangy dogs and cats.
There were taverners with trays of beer, and bakers with
armfuls of bread. There were boys carrying bundles of
kindling, men shouldering bolts of cloth, donkeys loaded
with fruit, and oxen heaving tree trunks.

She heard friendly conversations and noisy fights, the
bicker of women, the banter of traders, the whicker of
horses and the snort of boars. She smelled spilt wine,
warm dung, live chickens and ripe cheese; molten metal
from the blacksmith's forge and raw meat from the
butcher's stall. There was smoke from the fires, steam
from the pots they heated, and a constant drip from the
washing lines which hung overhead. Rome was noisy,
tatty, filthy, smelly, hot and dusty and the most exciting
place that Doris had ever been.

The face appeared suddenly.

It was wizened and toothless, spiked with coarse
black whiskers and framed in a grubby shawl. Doris
flinched when the hag held out a claw-like hand, but the

litter bearers made no effort to shoo the woman off, and Doris was appalled when Caesar leant forward to speak to her.

'So, Spurinna,' he said mysteriously. 'The ides of March is arrived.'

'Aye,' the hag hissed back. 'Arrived, and not yet over. It is but halfway through.'

'Spurinna?' Doris repeated to herself. 'Is this the soothsayer that Cassius mentioned?'

Spurinna tugged at her shawl and clasped it under her chin with a gnarled fist.

'And therefore I say again,' she hissed, 'beware the ides! Beware!'

She turned away, but even as she melted into the crowds and disappeared, her sinister warning echoed in her wake, 'Beware the ides! The ides!'

Caesar and Doris had almost reached their destination, the Theatre of Pompey, when they were approached yet again, this time by a well-dressed gentleman. Caesar obviously knew the man, and said 'hello' to him, but then apologized and explained that he couldn't stop to talk because he was running late for a meeting of the Senate.

The man nodded understandingly and glanced nervously over his shoulder. Then he delved into his sleeve and withdrew a loosely tied papyrus scroll. He passed it through the side of the litter and urged Caesar to read it immediately. Caesar promised he would, said good bye to the man, and laid the unopened scroll on top of his other papers.

When Caesar entered the theatre with Doris, the gentlemen of the Senate were chatting to one another in huddled groups. Some were standing, others were sitting down or lolling across the benches, but they all got to their feet when they saw Caesar.

Everyone bowed their heads respectfully and Caesar nodded in response. Then he marched briskly to his throne, put Doris on the floor, laid his papers beside her and sat down. He adjusted and smoothed his toga and purple cloak then patted his knee, and Doris jumped onto it. Most of the three-hundred or so senators took seats too, but a handful left their places and gathered in a semi-circle around the throne. Some pressed so close that Doris could smell their breath and hear their heartbeats. Never having been to a meeting of the Senate, she had no idea whether this was normal behaviour or not. Caesar didn't seem concerned, but Doris was uneasy. The heat of the men's bodies and the beads of sweat gathering on their foreheads was beginning to make her feel claustrophobic and panicky.

She had just snuggled deeper into Caesar's lap when a sudden breeze whipped through the theatre and lifted some of his papers off the floor. Doris watched them skitter and dance. She was glad of the distraction, especially when the ties of the scroll that Caesar had taken from the gentleman began to unravel. Doris leant over and peered at the scroll. It was too far away and too curled up for her to read, but she could see that it was written in her first language, Greek.

She left Caesar's lap and slid under the arm of his throne to the cool stone floor. Then she flattened the scroll with her paws and mouthed each character quietly to herself until she had strung them into words.

She soon realised why the gentleman had been so insistent that Caesar should read the letter. It was a warning, and it came straight to the point. Someone was going to try to kill Caesar, here and now, at this very meeting. Doris shook her head, partly to clear it but mostly in disbelief. When the enormity of what she'd read finally sank in, she struggled out from under the shadow of the throne and barked.

Caesar was so closely surrounded now that Doris couldn't see him. She had no idea whether he could see her, but what she *did* know was that she *had* to find a way to get him out of the theatre. She looked about, desperately searching for a way to get his attention. Once she'd done that, the rest would be easy. All she'd need do was head for the door and run like crazy. Caesar would be bound to follow.

There was a candelabra on either side of the throne. Each was the height of a man and had a solid metal base and a central stem which branched into five candle holders.

Doris took a few steps backwards and lined herself up with the midsection of the candelabra nearest her. Then she crouched low, like a cat, took a deep breath and flung herself forwards. She hit the candelabra head-on and it rocked promisingly but then settled back on its base. Doris sighed with disappointment and turned to make a second attempt. Just then, though, one of the candles wobbled in its holder and fell to the floor with a clatter. Caesar and the other men started and whipped round, the candle trundled across the marble floor, and Doris barked.

Her high voice bounced around the newly quiet chamber and Caesar stood up. Doris could see his face now. She looked straight at him and barked again. She could tell from his expression that he knew she wasn't being playful. He understood that she was trying to tell him something. He pushed his arms forward and sideways as if trying to swim through the surrounding men, but one of them lunged forward and wrenched the sacred purple cloak from his shoulders. Doris saw Caesar's mouth open in surprise, heard him gasp, and then felt a ripple of air as the cloak flopped onto the ground beside her.

She watched as the men forced Caesar away from the throne, into the open. She saw a flash of steel and realised that someone had drawn a dagger. She followed the men, snarling and snapping at their ankles and tugging frantically at their clothes, sandals and anything else she could get her teeth into.

More knives appeared.

They flailed about indiscriminately until Doris felt a sharp pain. She looked down and saw cherry red liquid seeping across the floor. The black flesh on one of her pads had been torn open. The sight of the blood made her dizzy. She'd seen blood before, but never her own.

Her paw was stinging now, and she was beginning to feel faint. She stood on three legs and let her foot dangle. Perhaps it was because of her sudden stillness, maybe it would have happened anyway, but for some reason one of the men suddenly turned his attention to her.

'Aw. Hurt your paw, have you?' he said gently.

He held out a hand and rubbed his fingers together as if offering a tit-bit, but Doris wasn't fooled. She tried to back away but the coldness of the marble floor on her injured paw made her flinch. She let out an involuntary squeal.

'Ha!' the man spat in a sudden change of tone. 'So precious you are, with your eastern mistress and your fancy collar!'

He raised his knife and charged. His mouth was wide open, his eyes wild. Doris squealed again, tucked her tail between her legs and tried to make for the shelter of the throne. Her paws skittered on the marble and she seemed to be going nowhere as the man lunged after her, slashing the air with his blade and cursing in Latin. She reached Caesar's fallen cloak and skidded onto it.

'Cassius!' she prayed. 'Help me, Cassius!'

The cloak bunched under her feet and slid across the floor, taking her with it. The man lunged again, caught the edge of the throne with his knife, and snapped his wrist unnaturally forwards. He screamed, the knife bounced onto the purple cloak, and the cloak, the knife and Doris skated under the throne.

The man lay down, rolled onto his side and thrust an arm

into Doris's hiding place. Doris didn't know whether he was after her or his knife, but both were out of his reach. She watched his hand grab blindly at thin air until he finally cursed again and went back to his friends.

Doris stayed where she was.

She could still see Caesar. At one point he turned her way. There was a deep gash across his face. It was pouring with frightening, living blood, like her paw. He caught sight of Doris and she looked steadily back at him and bared her teeth in her best rendition of a smile. She left the throne, stood on her hind legs and jabbed with her front paws like the prize boxers she'd seen in Alexandria. She wanted to will him to go on fighting but he had no weapon of his own. He was trying to defend himself with his stylus, but it was only a writing implement. It had been made for cutting into wax, not flesh.

When a young man stepped forward and thrust a dagger into Caesar's groin, Doris feared the worst. Caesar stumbled, then regained his balance and stared at the man. When he spoke it was with absolute calm and terrible sadness.

'And you too, my child,' he said.

Then he slid to the floor.

The assassins and the other senators fled, and Doris found herself alone in the theatre. At first she was unable to move and could do nothing but lie on the cold stone floor and blink in disbelief. Finally, she struggled to her feet and hobbled back to the throne.

Her paw was still stinging, but she hardly noticed that. She picked up the purple cloak with her teeth and dragged it to Caesar. When she reached him, she used her nose and paws as gently as she could to cover him up. Then, exhausted, numb and soaked in her own blood and that of her dead master, she lay down and howled.

CHAPTER FIFTEEN
Bo's House.
The 21st Century

'You don't have to talk about Caesar if you don't want to,' said Cavendish kindly.

'No,' Bo replied miserably. 'I don't.'

The spaniel put a comforting paw on her shoulder.

'It must have been terrible for Doris,' he added. 'Seeing Caesar die like that.'

Bo wondered how Cavendish knew that Doris had been at the theatre, but she didn't feel up to asking him. She knew from experience that she wouldn't get a straight answer, and she was in no mood to argue.

'Yes. Yes, it was,' was all she said.

She sighed.

'Caesar had a bad feeling about that day,' she added quietly. 'Everybody did. If only Decimus hadn't made him go to the meeting. If only Caesar had read the scroll. A gentleman gave it to him outside the theatre. It was a warning. It told him someone might try to kill him but he didn't even look at it. Doris did, though. She read it. She tried to get his attention. She was going to run out of the theatre so he'd follow her, but it didn't work.'

'Let me tell you something,' said Cavendish. 'It might make you feel better.'

'I doubt it.'

'Well, listen anyway,' Cavendish insisted, 'and you'll realise that there was nothing to be done or undone. Not by Doris, not by Decimus, not even by the man with the scroll.'

'Go on,' said Bo.

'One of Caesar's best friends was a man called Mark Antony,' Cavendish began. 'He was a cavalry commander.'

Bo tipped her head and Cavendish tried not to smile. He knew he'd got her attention. Bo liked cavalry commanders. When she'd been Mignonne in the days of King Charles I, she'd fallen a little in love with the king's own cavalry commander, Prince Rupert.

'Antony was immensely strong and very brave,' Cavendish continued. 'If he'd been at the meeting that day, there is no way the assassins would have attacked Caesar. And Antony should have been there, but the assassins waylaid him. Their plan worked, as it happens, but if it hadn't, if Antony had turned up at the theatre, they would simply have postponed things, and that's all. No one and nothing could have stopped them forever.'

'*But why?*' Bo wailed. 'Why did they have to kill Caesar?'

'Because they thought he was too powerful and too involved with Cleopatra.'

'Oh, no! Cleopatra!' Bo squealed. 'I'd completely forgotten about Cleopatra! She loved Caesar, too. She must have been distraught!'

'Of course she was distraught. But when you're the most powerful woman on earth you can't just collapse in a heap when something awful happens, however much you might feel like it. You have to pick yourself up and get on with life. Most of all, you have to show your enemies that you are still strong.'

'She was good at that,' said Bo.

Cavendish chuckled.

'You're getting to know her very well,' he said. 'Cleopatra did what she did best. She stayed calm and went home to Alexandria. By the time she got there, Rome was falling apart. The people were taking sides and fighting amongst themselves. Some were for Antony, some were for the assassins, and still others were for a young man called Octavian. It was a mess.'

'Octavian? Who's he? I've never *heard* of him.'

'Not many people had. But he had his supporters. Even *they* didn't know much about him, except that he was Caesar's great-nephew and legal heir, and that he lived in the countryside. He was also a bit of a swot and rather delicate.'

'He sounds wet,' said Bo disparagingly.

'Wet but very clever.'

'What about the assassins? One of them was a young man,' Bo remembered. 'He was the last person to stab Caesar. I'll never forget the way Caesar looked at him.'

'That was Brutus,' Cavendish nodded. 'Caesar loved Brutus. He'd treated him like a son, so for Brutus to do what he did was especially shocking. Brutus committed suicide, in the end, but thousands of others were caught and killed. Antony was on a mission. He hunted down anyone and everyone who'd been involved in the assassination, however loosely. It was a bloodbath.'

'Do you think Antony ever met Cleopatra? He could have told her all about it. It might have made her feel better to know that Caesar's assassins were dead.'

'She didn't need to be told. She kept in touch with what was going on. Octavian and Antony began to work together. They both knew they'd be stronger like that. When they'd defeated the assassins, they divided Rome's provinces between them. Antony got the eastern part. He knew the area well and had a good understanding of its languages and people. And yes, he did meet Cleopatra.'

'Then he must have met Doris, too,' Bo said. 'I wonder if she liked him.'

'I'm sure she did. Antony had been Caesar's best friend, remember?'

'Yes, but Caesar gave Doris hugs. Antony doesn't sound the hugging type.'

'You're *so* wrong about that, Bo. Antony was the best hugger ever. Antony hugged for Rome.'

CHAPTER SIXTEEN
The River Cyndus, Tarsus, Cilicia.
Summer 41BC

For her cruise down the Nile with Caesar, Cleopatra had selected a ship of sublime elegance, The State Barge.

This vessel was something else entirely.

She had bright purple sails, a golden poop and silver oars. Incense wafted from her hull, handmaidens dressed as sea nymphs posed against her rails, and there was a four-poster bed on her upper deck.

Doris sighed contentedly, wriggled out of Cleopatra's arms and shuffled to the end of the bed. She rolled onto her back and let her paws flop, then stared through the bed's translucent canopy and watched the sails billow against the sky. She closed her eyes for a moment and listened to the tick-ticking of rigging in the breeze, then flipped over and sat up.

To her left and right, hundreds of people had lined the river's banks. A few boys and young lads were running to keep level with the ship, but most of the crowd were just standing stock still and staring. They were literally open-mouthed. Their jaws had dropped to their chests, and their eyes were huge with awe and disbelief.

Aphrodite, the Goddess of Love, was floating past them on their very own river.

All gods had earthly guises. Some became animals, such as Sebek the crocodile. Others took human form, like Isis, who came to earth as The Queen, and Aphrodite, who came as herself. Aphrodite didn't need a flamboyant costume. She was the goddess of love, after all. So for Cleopatra, being Aphrodite was easy. All she had to do was lounge against a pile of cushions, look romantic and wear practically nothing.

Doris, on the other hand, was sporting a specially commissioned collar. It was meant to look like aphros, or sea foam, which was what Aphrodite was said to have been born out of, and was made of fine silver wire decorated with river-pearls and tiny blue diamonds.

Doris thought it rather pretty. Though she did feel a little overdressed, by comparison to her mistress.

Doris got to her feet and barked at the crowd, and they sank to their knees in adoration.

'Amuse them, Doris,' Cleopatra giggled from her cushions. 'You may take the choir with you.'

The choir consisted of little boys wearing Cupid costumes. Their pink wings had once belonged to real flamingos, and their solid silver bows had gold-tipped arrows.

Doris leapt down from the bed and trotted up to the Cupids, who shuffled into a line behind her. Then she and they set off on a tour around the decks, their seventh that day. Whilst the boys sang love songs in their high, treble voices, Doris pranced up and down and led them, conga-style, around the ship's rails. When she'd finished, she did a couple of twirls on her hind legs, the Cupids returned to their posts, and Doris went back to bed.

Evening approached, and the ship reached a still, mirror-like lake. Her sails were lowered, she was tied to a mooring, and hundreds of tiny lanterns were strung along her rails. By the time the sun went down, the whole ship was twinkling. It was as though she was made from the stars themselves, and the god-fearing folk who had followed her upriver were more mesmerized than ever.

Little did they know that the best was yet to come. Within a few hours, this magical ship would welcome aboard none other than the great god Dionysus, a.k.a. Mark Antony.

The local people loved Antony. To them, the dashing cavalry commander who ruled over them was not only a hero, but also the god Dionysus, Provider Of Joy, Wine And Drama. They had no concept that such an all-conquering God Of Fruitfulness might have the same pressing concerns as mere mortals like themselves. Nor did they understand that, like every Roman leader before him, Antony needed money and grain to pay and feed his soldiers. But Cleopatra understood. Antony might hold the power of Rome, but it was she who held the purse strings of the richest country in the world. Egypt needed the friendship and protection of Rome, Rome needed

Egypt's money. It was as simple as that. So Cleopatra had sailed the seas to meet with Antony, provide her own joy, wine and drama, and show him just how fabulously wealthy she was.

Menander was busy helping Cleopatra to dress for one of the most important nights of her life, so Doris left them to it and went to watch the finishing touches being put to the party room.

When she reached its threshold, she stopped dead in her tracks. The room's walls and ceiling had been covered in sheets of highly polished metal and these 'mirrors' reflected everything a hundred times over. Doris could see hundreds of poodles, hundreds of pieces of wonderful furniture, hundreds of servants and thousands of candles. She blinked, wandered to the centre of the floor and sat down.

She was surrounded by forty or more silk couches, each with its own table of jewelled goblets and dishes. There were brightly coloured cushions and elegant throws and many, many candles. Doris couldn't even begin to count how many. They were everywhere. They were spiked onto candelabras, fixed into wall sconces, peppered about on tables, and balanced in bowls suspended from the ceiling.

Doris sat quietly whilst the servants had a last rehearsal. Each of them carried a lighted taper to a different section of the room. Then, simultaneously and with perfect timing, they lit every wick within their reach. Within seconds, all the candles in the room were alight, and their tiny flames were multiplied in the mirrored walls. Their glittering reflections bounced off the room's gorgeous contents, and the jewels, gold and glass twinkled in all the colours of the rainbow.

Doris thought it the most beautiful sight she'd ever seen. Which was just as well, really, because Cleopatra had gone to a great deal of trouble to achieve it.

When Antony arrived at the ship, Doris kept her distance. Cleopatra needed Antony's friendship, and that was fine. Doris wouldn't dream of doing anything to jeopardise her mistress's plans, but she didn't need to follow suit. She would form her own opinion of Antony, do it in her own time, and act accordingly.

It was obvious from the start that Antony was very different from Caesar. True, he was tanned and well-muscled, as Caesar had been, but he was also very handsome, and young. He had soft brown eyes and a mane of thick, dark, curly hair, but he was less vain than Caesar, and a lot less pernickety. His clothes were neither neat nor well-pressed, and he soon removed the ivy wreath, symbol of the god Dionysus, from his head, something which Caesar would never have done. He also put down his Dionysiac wand, an ivy-clad fennel stalk topped with a pine cone, and didn't seem at all concerned when it rolled off the table onto the floor. He didn't appear to worry too much about what he ate, either, and washed down huge amounts of food with copious quantities of wine. He seemed kind, and Cleopatra clearly found him amusing, but he was also extremely noisy and unruly, and had a raucous laugh and a habit of banging his fist on the table.

Doris spent most of the party hiding under a chair.

On the following evening, Cleopatra threw a second party for Antony. Just before it was due to begin, Menander proudly carried an enamelled casket into Doris's salon.

'This will cheer you up,' he said as he sat down and opened the casket's lid. 'I made it specially for you.'

He delved into the casket and gently removed a headdress. It was made from the leaves, stem and purple grapes of a vine, and was sprinkled with a fine blue dust which gave it a sparkling sheen.

'I dipped it in melted wax and then sifted powdered lapis over the top,' Menander explained with pride. 'It will look di*vine* in candlelight,' he giggled at the pun, 'and the wax will preserve it a while. Here, let's brush you out and try it on.'

He settled Doris in front of her mirror and began to tease out the knots in her ears.

'Sitting on the deck in the wind's what does this,' he said. 'The breeze, the salty air.'

Doris winced as he tackled a particularly matted clump.

'Sorry,' he said. 'You know, poppet, Mr. Antony is a very brave and famous man. He's a *cavalry commander*.'

'Yes,' mumbled Doris. 'I know.'

Menander paused, selected a new brush, and fluffed

up the fur on Doris's head.

'I know you miss Caesar,' he continued. 'We all do. But he and Mr. Antony were great friends, and Caesar would have wanted you to get along with each other. Your mistress wants it too. That's why she asked me to make this headdress for you.'

Menander reached out for some pins, put several in his mouth, and began to fix the headdress.

'Antony will be her guest of honour again tonight,' he explained through the pins, 'and this vine will especially please him. For he is Dionysus, a mighty conqueror, Lord of Asia and God of Wine. Hence the grapes. There! How pretty you look! I am to wait here with you until Antony arrives. Then I will take you to him. You might come to love him, Doris. If only you would try.'

'When I'm ready,' Doris growled. 'I'll try when I'm ready.'

When Charmion came to say that Cleopatra had asked for Doris, Menander carried Doris to the party room.

Just outside the door, he paused.

'Look at me,' he said as he turned Doris's chin in his hand. 'I want you to think of Caesar,' he said. 'I want you to remember that the greatest Roman who ever lived was putty in your hands. Remember his words, Doris. Veni, Vidi, Vici.'

'I came, I saw, I conquered,' Doris translated.

'You can conquer, too,' Menander urged. 'You can conquer anything and anyone you want.'

He nodded to the guards to open the door and then he

stepped into the party.

'Look at Mark Antony. See how he drinks and laughs? He's a softy, really. You conquered Caesar, Doris. Conquering Antony should be easy.'

He set Doris down on the floor and gave her a gentle shove.

She began to walk across the room.

Its beauty was dizzying, as were her wobbling legs.

She gazed steadfastly ahead until she spotted her mistress. Cleopatra was laughing and touching Antony on the shoulder.

Doris turned and glanced back at Menander for reassurance.

He was still standing in the doorway, but now he was swinging one arm as if to shoo her along.

'Go!' he mouthed.

'Doris!' Cleopatra called. 'Come over here, Doris!'

'Antony,' she said as Doris approached. 'This is my Doris. Doris, this is Antony.'

Doris and Antony's eyes locked.

'Most famous Doris Of The Lovely Hair,' said Antony with a gracious bow of his head. 'Great favourite of my great friend, Caesar. It is a pleasure and an honour to meet you.'

'Good response,' thought Doris.

'I missed you last night,' Antony added. 'Were you not here?'

'She was,' Cleopatra replied, 'but she did not show herself.'

She darted a disapproving look at Doris but then

picked up a roasted dormouse.

'I think she was a little nervous,' she continued as she passed the mouse to Antony. 'Try her with this.'

'It'll take a bit more than *that*,' Doris muttered.

Then she noticed that Antony's hand was shaking.

She crept closer to his couch, stretched her neck and took the dormouse from his fingers.

'Well met at last!' Cleopatra said delightedly. 'You two will become firm friends, I am sure of it.'

Dinner that night boasted some of the world's most sought-after and expensive delicacies. In addition to the dormice, there were sows' udders, Black Sea caviar, flamingo tongues and quail, and Doris sampled them all, straight from Antony's hand.

CHAPTER SEVENTEEN
The following morning

Early next morning, and whilst Cleopatra was still asleep, Doris lay on the ship's upper deck and thought about things. She was badly missing her old friends Caesar and Cassius. Most of all she missed having someone to talk to.

'I know he's a cat,' she muttered to herself, 'and a big one, at that. But Cassius is the only one I can really chat with. My ma still misses Caesar, but she no longer cries at night the way she used to do. She used to sob into my fur and tell me how much she missed him, how lonely she was. She doesn't do that so much nowadays. She's making friends with Antony, and it's me who's feeling lonely.'

Doris immediately felt guilty.

She knew the queen could not afford to mope about and hark back to old times. Her very survival depended on staying sharp. She had to be canny, and that had always meant making friends with the most powerful man in the world.

Once, that man had been Caesar.

Now it was Antony.

Caesar's day was over. Cleopatra had come to terms with that, and now Doris must do the same. She might be pampered, but she wasn't spoilt or stupid. She needed friends, too. She knew she must make an effort with Antony.

The theme for the next party was roses, and Doris approached the party room with new determination, a garland of roses around her neck and a single bloom behind each ear. She'd intended to rush across the room and jump enthusiastically onto Antony's lap, but she hadn't known that the floor was carpeted with petals. They were piled so deep they reached her knees, and she had to concentrate hard and high-step to get through them.

'Hah!' Antony exclaimed when she finally made it onto his knee. 'Here is my new friend, Doris Of The Lovely Hair! I was wondering when the party would start!'

He slapped his thigh.

'Antony has a little surprise for you, Doris,' Cleopatra said. 'He's been barely able to contain himself.'

'Shall we?' Antony asked. 'Yes! Why not?'

He raised a hand in the air and snapped his fingers.

'Wheel it on!' he roared, collapsing into peals of laughter and reaching for his goblet of wine. 'Wheel on the surprise!'

A trumpet sounded, and Cleopatra's guests fell silent and turned in their chairs as a pair of curtains swished apart at the far end of the room. Beyond them were six male slaves and a huge box. The slaves were dressed as zebras. They had real zebra tails and real zebra heads and their bodies were painted with black and white stripes which blended perfectly with their zebra skin loincloths. The box stood between them. It was made of papyrus and tied up like a present, with a wide silk ribbon and a big floppy bow.

The 'zebras' hee-hawed and pawed the ground with their coconut-shell hooves, and Antony pointed to the box.

''Tis only paper, Doris,' he said. 'Go punch it open! See what lies within.'

Doris bounced onto the floor and trotted towards the box. She stepped up to it, smelled a warm, familiar smell, and plunged one of her paws straight through the delicate papyrus.

The paper crackled and crumpled and collapsed in a heap, and Cassius leapt out of it and gave Doris a gentle shove with his head.

'Don't eat the zebras,' Doris giggled. 'Where've you come from?'

'Lately? Rome,' the lion replied as he and Doris meandered over to Antony and Cleopatra. 'Caesar left me to Antony in his will.'

'Oh *that's* nice,' said Doris. 'I hope it means we'll see more of each other. I've missed you, Cassius.'

'Me too. But listen to this! You'll never guess who I saw in Rome...'

'Um...Octavian?'

'Yes, but someone else, too.'

'No idea. Give me a clue.'

Cassius curled his upper lip, fluttered his eyelashes and fanned his nose with one of his paws.

'*No!*' Doris squealed. 'Not *Polygnotus!*'

'The very same.'

'So you were right, Cassius. He *did* escape the crocs,' said Doris, amazed.

'Well, most of him did. He's lost an arm.'

'And you've seen him?'

'Yes, indeed. Rather more than I'd have wished, in fact. He's managed to ingratiate himself into Octavian's household and is slimier than ever. At first I wondered if it was Cleopatra's doing, that maybe she'd sent him there as a spy.'

'I doubt it,' Doris said. 'She never liked him. She hasn't mentioned him since the day he jumped off The State Barge. I'm sure she knows he had something to do with the poisoned knife. She'd certainly never trust him with a secret, even if it was Octavian's.'

Cassius nodded.

'I thought that's what you'd say.'

'So what's Octavian like?' Doris asked.

'Sickly looking,' Cassius replied. 'They say he never turns up for battles, he's always too ill. But he's very shrewd, extremely clever and calculating. Antony thought he was a bit of an upstart at first, but he's learning to watch his back. I think Octavian could be very dangerous.'

'Oh, dear,' Doris sighed. 'Wha...?'

The ceiling had been tented with widths of fine netting

filled with rose petals, but now someone had whisked the netting away, and the rose petals were spiralling to the floor like a million pink butterflies.

The parties continued. Each was more elaborate than the last and, at the end of one of them, Antony remarked that Cleopatra must have reached the very pinnacle of extravagance. Surely even *she* couldn't throw a more splendid and expensive evening than the one they'd just enjoyed? He meant it as a compliment, but Cleopatra took it as a challenge and made a bet with him. She wagered that the next party would cost her an *obscene* amount of money.

On the following night, more fabulous foods and wines were served, and the musicians, jugglers and dancers performed their hearts out. Yet at the end of the evening Antony declared that, although the meal and its surroundings had indeed been very beautiful, there had been nothing to make this party stand out from all the others. Cleopatra, he said, had lost her bet.

Doris caught Cassius's eye and looked heavenwards.

'*Big* mistake,' she mouthed.

Cleopatra glanced sideways at Antony.

'Not so fast, my darling,' she purred. 'Not so fast.'

'Here we go,' said Doris.

Cleopatra snapped her fingers and Menander stepped forward with a golden goblet in one hand and a flask of vinegar in the other.

'What the...?' Cassius asked.

'I've no idea,' Doris replied, 'but it's bound to be good. Watch.'

On Cleopatra's cue, and with a theatrical flourish, Menander poured a small amount of the vinegar into the goblet. Cleopatra then gently removed one of her extremely rare and excruciatingly expensive Indian Ocean pearl earrings.

Doris folded her paws over her head.

'Oh no, ma. Don't do that,' she groaned. 'Don't!'

Cleopatra held the pearl above the goblet, counted aloud to five, and then dropped the precious jewel into the vinegar.

'She's done it, Doris,' said Cassius.

There was an awed silence whilst everyone waited and watched to see if Cleopatra would hold her nerve. She took the goblet and swirled its contents to make sure that the pearl had completely dissolved. Then she fixed Antony with a steady gaze. When she knew she had his undivided attention, she threw back her head, drank the precious liquid down in one and slammed the goblet on the table.

Point made.

Not long after that little incident, Antony and Cassius left the ship for the last time, and Cleopatra and Doris prepared to go home. As the ship upped-anchor and slipped away from its mooring, Antony and Cassius stood on the bank and waved.

Cleopatra held Doris aloft.

'Wave back then, Doris,' she said, taking hold of

Doris's wrist.

'Good bye!' Antony called.

'Good bye!' roared Cassius.

''Bye!' Doris barked.

'I shall miss them,' said Cleopatra wistfully.

'So shall I,' thought Doris.

CHAPTER EIGHTEEN
Bo's House.
The 21st Century

'Doris was crazy about Antony,' Bo told Cavendish, 'and Antony was crazy about her, and Cleopatra. He was also quite tipsy a lot of the time.'

Cavendish chuckled.

'Octavian would have been proud of you,' he said.

'Why's that?'

'Because Roman society was full of uptight prudish snobs. The chattering classes had a field-day. They decided that Antony was a drunken ne'er-do-well who'd fallen under the spell of a wicked, eastern queen. That suited Octavian very well indeed.'

'Cleopatra wasn't wicked!' protested Bo.

'No, she wasn't,' Cavendish agreed. 'It was pure propaganda. Octavian was a scheming politician, and a good one. He was also becoming ever more powerful. Antony should have seen that. He should have left Tarsus and gone straight back to his work in Rome, but he didn't. He followed Doris and Cleopatra to Alexandria instead.'

'Oh goody,' Bo trilled. 'He makes Cleopatra happy.

She really lets her hair down when he's around.'

'It wasn't really "goody", Bo. Antony had worked hard to get where he was. He needed to be seen in Rome. He risked losing everything if he spent too much time away.'

'World domination isn't everything,' said Bo. 'You have to live a little, too.'

'Antony and Cleopatra knew that,' Cavendish nodded. 'For all their ambition, they knew that life was for living. Antony may not have had Caesar's manners or Cleopatra's quick wit, but he was genuine, honourable and kind. Those are rare virtues in someone so famous and powerful. He and Cleopatra had good times together, and it wasn't always about expensive parties. They had many riotous nights when they spent hardly any money at all. You should go back and see that. There was one particular time...'

'Why that one?' Bo interjected.

'What?'

'Why that night? What's so special about it? Something's going to happen, isn't it? Is Doris going to be poisoned again?'

'No.'

'Stabbed?'

'No. Now stop it. Close your eyes and try to imagine Cleopatra's bedchamber in Alexandria. The queen is naked, and Menander is rubbing her all over with soil and dust. The two of them are giggling. Doris is lying on the bed and watching their antics when the door opens, and in walks Antony.'

CHAPTER NINETEEN
The Royal Palace, Alexandria, Egypt.
Winter 41BC

Antony and Cleopatra had been having fun and games in Alexandria. They'd gone swimming at the harbour, fishing in the Nile and hunting on the plains. They'd thrown dinner parties and card nights, and they'd visited the palace gymnasium so that Antony could practice his swordsmanship. He'd been practicing his Greek, too, and had even taken to wearing Greek clothes. Antony was loving Alexandrian life, and had made sure to include Doris and Cassius in *almost* all he did. One exception was his secret, night-time forays. He liked to soak up the city's atmosphere and mingle with the crowds without being recognised. To do this, he had to go undercover.

Doris was lying on Cleopatra's bed, watching Menander. He'd spent the past hour transforming Cleopatra into a slave-girl. Now that he was almost finished, there was a tap on the door and Antony entered the room. He was wearing everyday Grecian clothes and leading Cassius on the end of a rope.

Cleopatra took one look at the lion.

'Antony,' she giggled. 'You cannot take that onto the streets! Who will believe you are an ordinary man if you have with you the great cat of Julius Caesar and Mark Antony?'

'I wasn't intending to take him,' Antony replied. 'I brought him here to keep Doris company.'

'But Doris is coming with *us*!' Cleopatra exclaimed.

Doris pricked her ears.

'Now that really *is* ridiculous,' Antony laughed. 'Doris is even more famous than Cassius!'

Antony and Cleopatra went on bickering good-naturedly until they agreed that both animals must stay behind.

Doris drummed her paws on the bed.

'Hippopotami!' she swore. 'I want to go with *them*.'

'Not possible,' said Cassius as he jumped up beside her. 'Never mind. We'll have a quiet night in. What's Menander doing to your mistress?'

'Making her look like a slave-girl.'

'He's *good*. No one would ever know it was her.'

'At least she's got some clothes on now. She was stark naked a few minutes ago. Menander's smeared dirt all over her. He's even rubbed sand in her hair and made her dig her fingernails into a basinful of wet soil.'

Antony took Cleopatra by the hand.

'Come then, my little slave. Follow me, but be sure to keep a respectful distance. Five paces will suffice.'

'Very funny,' Cleopatra giggled.

The couple set off on their caper, Menander began to tidy up, and Doris and Cassius settled down for a snooze.

'Cleopatra's only *pretending* to be a slave,' said Doris, deadpan. 'She's done it before. She'll probably speak Troglodyte, too. That'll make things even *more* authentic.'

'I doubt that,' Cassius mused.

'No, really she will. She speaks loads of languages. Ethiopian, Hebrew, Aramaic, Syriac, Median, Parthian, Egyptian, Greek, some Latin and some Troglodyte.'

'Troglodytes live in caves, Doris. I think you mean Trogodyte. It's an Egyptian tribal language.'

'Oh.'

'I heard Antony and Cleopatra talking today...'

'Me too.'

'No. I mean *talking*. You weren't there. I think you'd gone to the gardens. It was a very serious talk, Doris. Very serious. Did you know that Antony is planning to invade Parthia?'

'Caesar's Parthia?'

'The very same,' Cassius confirmed. 'So I don't think the fun will last much longer.'

Menander had finished his tidying and was heading for the door with the basin of soil he'd used to dirty Cleopatra's fingernails.

'I'm just going to take this outside,' he said.

Doris stood up and shook herself.

'Menander's left the door open,' she said. 'And if what you say is true, and the fun's about to end, then I'm going to make the most of it. I want to see what Antony gets up to on these forays of his. Especially since this time he's taken my mistress with him. I don't care what they said, I'm going to follow them. '

'Oh, no, Doris. Please don't...'

CHAPTER TWENTY

Doris soon picked up Antony and Cleopatra's scent.

She followed it along the palace corridors, through chambers and ante-rooms, out by a servants' door, down marble steps and across the gardens to the gates. When she reached the Canopic she turned down a side street and spotted them at last.

She hung back.

Ducking and diving, she tracked Antony and Cleopatra as closely as she dared whilst they knocked on doors and ran away laughing, tripped people up or tapped them on the shoulder and looked away. Finally, they stopped at a food stall, and Doris heard them order bread and tuna and two spiced beers.

She was still watching from the opposite side of the street when a huddle of people gathered in front of her and blocked her view. She shuffled from side to side and finally managed to squeeze between their legs, but by then Antony and Cleopatra had gone.

Doris was way out of the small patch of Alexandria that was familiar to her. The palace had ample gardens for her to walk and play in, and the few strolls she'd taken beyond them had always been with Menander or Charmion. Even then, they'd only covered a few streets.

Now she was lost. Alexandria seemed dark and shadowy, the wisps of sea mist creeping around her were disorientating, and she was getting damp and cold.

She saw a burning brazier and began to walk towards it, hoping to warm herself up before trying to get home.

She heard a movement somewhere ahead of her, and hugged the wall, afraid of coming face to face with one of Alexandria's horrible harbour rats. But it was only a man. He emerged from a doorway further down the street, and she breathed a sigh of relief and began to follow him towards the brazier. She was desperate for its warmth, but the closer she got to the man, the more uneasy she felt.

She dropped back and sat down on the paving stones, and as she did so the wind changed direction. She raised her nose and smelled a distinctive, cloying perfume. The man stepped into the light of a street lamp. His scent had been a clue, but now his identity was affirmed by the stump of his missing arm.

Polygnotus.

Doris's first instinct was to run, but when two other men appeared and greeted the eunuch, her curiosity got the better of her. She noticed an arched niche cut into the wall further down the street. It had probably once held a statue, and Doris decided it was the perfect place from which to eavesdrop.

Hugging the wall, keeping low to the ground, she ran

to the niche and darted into it. She could hear Polygnotus and the two men, now. They were speaking in Latin, but their voices were too hushed for Doris to make out what they were saying. Then one of the men raised his voice.

'That is for Octavian to decide!' he barked.

'And the gods to bestow,' the other added.

'That was not the agreement!' Polygnotus snapped. 'You *promised* you'd pay the first instalment tonight.'

'And *you* promised information,' the first man growled.

He took a dagger from under his cloak and held it to Polygnotus's throat.

'Tell us something worth hearing,' he challenged.

Then he spat on the ground at Polygnotus's feet, sheathed the dagger and set off down the street with his friend.

Polygnotus stood alone in the dark.

His shoulders were hunched and his remaining hand was raised to his mouth. He seemed to be trembling, but Doris couldn't have cared less. She didn't feel sorry for him. She just wished he'd move on so she could leave the niche and get herself to the brazier.

Without thinking, she flopped onto the ground to wait things out. Almost instantly, she felt something heave beneath her. She squealed, the thing squealed too, and Doris leapt sideways as a massive rat shot between her legs.

Polygnotus heard the noise and spun round.

'Who's there?' he asked nervously.

Doris prepared to flee, but a light shone in her eyes and for a moment she was blinded. A man was walking fast towards her, carrying a lantern.

By then, Polygnotus had recognised her.

'Stop!' he shouted at the startled man.

Then, more calmly, and with a false laugh, he added, 'No need for alarm, just don't allow that dog to run past you.'

The man held his lantern aloft.

'That looks like Cleopatra's Doris,' he said incredulously. 'Is it? Is that Doris Of The Lovely Hair?'

'Yes,' Polygnotus replied as he grabbed Doris by the tail.

The man gasped and sank to his knees. He dropped his lantern, tucked his head to his chest and pushed his hands along the ground.

'Hail, Doris!' he moaned.

He straightened his upper body and stretched his arms high above his head.

'Hail, Doris!' he repeated.

'Get up, get up!' Polygnotus screamed at him. 'Get up and help me lift her.'

'No,' the man said, shaking his head between his perpendicular arms. 'No, no, no. I cannot touch her. I am but a humble fisherman. I cannot touch Doris The Divine, Pet Of Isis, The Supreme Goddess Of...'

'Pick her up, you fool, or I shall inform the queen that you refused to help rescue her beloved companion from a night of cold and loneliness.'

Doris squirmed and wriggled, but Polygnotus's one

and only hand seemed to have garnered new strength. It was no longer weak and spidery, but had her tail in an iron grasp. She bared her teeth, snarled and contorted herself. She would happily have bitten Polygnotus, but however hard she tried she wasn't able to reach any part of him. Polygnotus was snarling too, and issuing threats and expletives to the fisherman who was now even more hesitant to touch Doris, and was beginning to back away.

Until that point, Doris and the men had been too engrossed to notice that the sky was glowing with a new, smoky-orange tint.

Now they heard chanting.

'Do-*RIS!* Do-*RIS!*'

The chanting grew louder and the glow turned to burning flames. The fisherman whipped round, Doris and Polygnotus stopped their snarling, and all three turned to stare. Crossing the end of the street was a party of palace servants carrying torches.

'Do-*RIS!* Do-*RIS!*'

'Here!' the fisherman called. '*STOP*! Over here! She's over here!'

He scooped up his lantern and raced up towards the search party, and Polygnotus let go of Doris's tail as if it were a blazing torch itself, then scuttled away before anyone could recognise him.

When Doris got back to Cleopatra's salon, Menander and Cassius were waiting for her. Menander had warmed the bed with heated stones and ordered a bowl of hot, hippo liver gravy.

'Don't you *ever* do that again!' he scolded.

Doris had never seen him so furious.

'I'm going to fetch your gravy now,' he added as he wrapped a rug around her, 'and you are not to move a muscle. Cassius? I'm relying on you to make sure she stays put. When I get back, we'll wait up together 'til your ma and Master Antony come home.'

Doris stared at him.

'Surely they're not still *out*?' she muttered. 'Good grief! What have they being *doing* all this time?'

'I was hoping *you'd* tell *me* that,' said Cassius when Menander had left the room. 'And by the way, why is it that you get heated stones and hippo gravy for misbehaving, whereas I get nothing for doing what I'm told?'

'Never mind about that,' Doris giggled. 'Listen to this!'

She told Cassius what she'd seen in the back streets of Alexandria, and asked him what he thought Polygnotus was up to.

'Who knows?' Cassius replied. 'Spying for Octavian, maybe. But it won't do him any good.'

'How so?'

'Because he'll never hear anything of any value. He can't get close enough to Antony or the queen. With any luck he'll give up soon and go elsewhere.'

Cassius paused.

'On the *other* hand,' he added with a twinkle in his eye, 'if he were to come up with something *really* juicy, he might bypass his mates in Alexandria and go straight to Octavian in Rome. Which would get him out of *our* hair.'

'But you've just said there's no chance of him hearing something juicy...'

'True. We'll just have to hope he disappoints his contacts so much that they murder him. Now *there's* a thought...'

'*You* can't kill him!' Doris wailed. 'If *you* killed him, they'd have you put *down*!'

She paused.

'You'd be a *man-eater*,' she added with undisguised glee.

'Hardly,' snorted Cassius. 'Anyway, Antony would never have me put me down. Especially not for Polygnotus.'

Cleopatra and Antony arrived home in the early hours. They were so elated and tired and drunk that they didn't seem to notice that Cassius and Doris were already lying on the bed. They collapsed in a heap on top of their pets, and Menander left the room and quietly closed the door behind him.

CHAPTER TWENTY-ONE
The following day

Menander returned at noon.

Cassius and Doris had extricated themselves by then, and had moved onto the floor. Both were fast asleep on their backs with their paws flopping in the air and a blissful look on their faces.

'Time to get up now, you two,' Menander said softly. 'Quick, quick! Let's go see Demetrius.'

He prodded Cassius who rolled onto his side with a grunt, sat up, and yawned.

'Come on, Doris,' the lion purred, 'it's cocktail time.'

Whenever Antony and Cleopatra were expected to wake up with hangovers, Demetrius made them a special curative cocktail. The basic ingredients for this were cabbage and egg yolk. These were considered the best antidotes for the hangover, but almond, pistachio, honey, apricot and a dash of mixed spice were added for flavour. Demetrius ground all of this into a mush and then tipped the whole lot into an emulsion of goat's milk, beer and palm oil. The result looked, and probably tasted, disgusting, but Antony and Cleopatra swore by it, and always drank it down in one, holding their noses and competing with each other to drain their cups.

The cocktail was ready and waiting when Menander, Cassius and Doris arrived at the kitchen.

'Here we are,' Demetrius said as he handed a jug and two cups to Menander. 'They tell me that Doris was lost last night.'

'That's true,' Menander replied. 'I had to send out a search party.'

Demetrius picked up a clay-baked crocodile claw and offered it to Cassius.

'I was asleep at the time,' the chef continued, 'I went to bed early so I could rise at dawn to meet with one of my fishermen. He specialises in morays and congas.'

'Eels,' said Menander with a shudder.

Demetrius nodded.

'Slippery sorts, they are. It was the fisherman who told me about Doris. He was there when the search party found her.'

'Then it was he who handed her over! I hope they thanked him properly.'

'He's not worried about that. He could see how relieved they were to find Doris, but they rushed off before he could tell them something.'

Demetrius paused and handed Doris a chunk of antelope heart.

'He and Doris were not alone. There was a eunuch with them. He had Doris by the tail. He asked the fisherman to help him lift her. He couldn't do it himself because she was trying to bite him...'

'I doubt that,' Menander scoffed.

'...she was trying to bite him, and he couldn't fight her off and lift her at the same time because he only had one arm.'

Menander started.

'No,' he said. 'Surely not. Polygnotus is in Rome. Master Antony has seen him there. That's how we learned he's alive. It's how we know about his arm.'

'*I* don't know of another one-armed eunuch, do you?'

'No,' said Menander. 'I don't.'

He glanced at Doris.

'Do you think he was trying to kidnap her?' he asked. 'Did the searchers find her just in time?'

'Who knows? The fisherman certainly thought he was acting strangely. Keep an eye on Doris, Menander. Make sure she doesn't go out on her own again.'

'As if,' Doris sighed.

Doris and Cassius followed Menander back to the queen's apartments, where they found Cleopatra and Antony up and dressed.

They had dismissed their servants and handmaidens and were standing alone in a small, private salon.

'Ah, good' said Antony when he saw the cocktail. 'Sustenance at last.'

Menander poured the drink, and Antony and Cleopatra picked up their cups, held their noses and swallowed.

Then they sat down at low table and turned their attention to a map. Menander stepped discreetly to the back of the room, but Doris and Cassius sidled up to the table.

'Where's that?' Doris asked as she examined the map.

'Syria and Mesopotamia,' Cassius replied.

'That's funny,' said Doris, puzzled, 'I always thought they were east of here.'

'They are. You're looking at them upside down.'

Doris tipped her head sideways.

'Oh yes,' she said. 'So I am.'

She walked round the table and jumped onto Cleopatra's knee just as Antony dipped a bamboo reed into a pot of ink.

'We begin by going this way,' he said as he drew a left to right horizontal line on the map. 'Out through Egypt's eastern border. Then...'

He pushed the pen away from him and slightly further right.

'...north through Syria. That gets us to Zeugma. So far, so good. Now,' he added, moving his pen sharply right again, 'to go directly east is by far the easiest option.'

He underscored this latest line.

'By *far* the easiest,' he repeated. 'And the quickest too. But I'm not going to do that! *Oh*, no. I'm going to let the Parthians *think* that's my plan, but I shall do something else entirely. I am going to come at them, not

from the west, but from the north!'

He flung the map aside and it slid across the floor and disappeared under a couch.

'Where's the other one?' he asked. 'Where's the map of Armenia?'

'In the next room,' Cleopatra replied.

'Then wait here,' said Antony. 'I'll fetch it and show you what I mean.'

'No, I'll come through, darling,' said Cleopatra, 'I'll be with you shortly.'

As Antony left through a side door, a pair of guards arrived at the salon's main entrance. Menander went to see what they wanted, and they told him that Polygnotus was at the palace gates requesting an audience with the queen.

'What is it, Menander?' Cleopatra asked. 'Did I hear the name Polygnotus? Do they mean Polygnotus the eunuch? I thought I'd seen the last of him! What does he want?'

'He says he has news of Doris, Your Majesty,' Menander related.

'Doris? But Doris is here,' said the queen.

'He says he has news about last night,' one of the guards called out.

Cleopatra waved a hand impatiently.

'Tell him, no,' she said. 'I don't want to see him. Tell him to go away. Menander, dear?'

'Yes, mistress?' Menander replied.

'Please take Doris and Cassius for a walk in the grounds. And don't let Doris out of your sight.'

'Yes, mistress.'

Cleopatra swept out of the room to join up with Antony, and Cassius turned to Doris.

'Do something to distract Menander,' the lion growled. 'I want to get that map out from under the couch.'

'Why?' Doris asked.

'You'll see. Be quick, Doris. Run away or something.'

Menander opened the door and called Doris and Cassius to his side, but both animals ignored him. Cassius stayed where he was, and Doris charged through the door and raced along the corridor towards the gardens. Whilst Menander rushed after her, screaming her name and pleading with her to stop, Cassius crawled under the couch and retrieved the map.

Doris kept running until she heard Cassius bounding up behind her. By then, Menander had caught up too.

'What have you got there?' the eunuch asked breathlessly. 'No, no, you can't have that. That's Antony's map.'

He reached out and tried to take the map from Cassius's mouth but the lion shook his mane and trotted purposefully away.

'Oh, well,' Menander sighed. 'I don't suppose it matters. It's not as though it gives away a great military secret. On the contrary, it shows what Antony *won't* do, not what he will.'

163

Cassius maintained a steady trot, completely ignored all calls to turn down this path or that, and forced Menander and Doris to follow him.

'He's heading for the gates,' Menander said at one point. 'Now why is he doing that?'

'Because he's *very* clever,' muttered Doris, who'd suddenly realised what the lion was up to.

Once in sight of the gates, Cassius stopped. He raised his nose and flattened his ears as the sea breeze lifted his mane and fluttered the map in his mouth. Then he swished his tail from side to side and growled softly.

A group of guards was standing on the far side of the gates. In their centre, screeching abuse and gesticulating towards Cleopatra's apartments, was Polygnotus.

Cassius walked on slowly, then bounded forward. The sudden movement caught the attention of Polygnotus, who looked up and saw Cassius apparently running off with a map whilst Menander tried to stop him. Polygnotus spat a last few curses at the guards, slunk back from the gates, and disappeared.

'Hippos!' Doris swore. 'It hasn't worked. He's seen Menander and taken off.'

But Cassius knew differently.

He bypassed the gates, swerved left, and followed the wall which separated the palace compound from the rest of the city. The wall was long, high and extremely thick, but it was no barrier to the lion's excellent sense of smell. This told him that Polygnotus was doing exactly what he'd hoped for. He was heading towards the place where the wall had one, tiny flaw.

'Windy Corner' was so named because it was the meeting point of several strong crosswinds. These whipped in from the sea and forced silt and sand against the harbour side of the wall. This caused a mound which could build so rapidly and get so high that the wall could be breached simply by scrambling up it. The fault was common knowledge in Alexandria, but Cassius had been told about it by Doris. She'd remembered Caesar ordering the silt to be cleared away to keep the palace safe during the Alexandrian Wars. Now, though, it was peacetime, the work was done less regularly, and the problem recurred in periods of high tides and wintry winds, such as there'd been lately.

By the time Doris and Menander caught up with Cassius, he'd already reached 'Windy Corner', and was standing in the lee of the wall with the map still in his mouth.

'What are you going to do?' Doris asked him.

Cassius rolled his eyes.

'Oh. Sorry. I see you can't talk right now,' Doris giggled.

She sniffed.

'I can smell Polygnotus,' she said. 'He's climbing the mound.'

Cassius nodded.

'You're not going to let him *in*, are you?'

Cassius shook his head and rolled his eyes again. This time he fixed them, very deliberately, at the top of the wall.

Doris wrinkled her nose.

'I don't understand,' she said.

Cassius turned until he was facing into the wind and the map began to flap and tug away from him.

'Oh! I've got it!' Doris barked, just as four fingers spidered over the wall. 'He's there, Cassius! I can see his hand. All you have to do now is wait for a big gust and then let go!'

Cassius nodded tolerantly.

When the ideal gust came, the lion opened his mouth and released the map. The wind carried it straight to the top of the wall and beyond, but then it caught a downdraught and began to float. Doris and Cassius stared upward as the map hovered, going nowhere, and Polygnotus's hand snatched at empty air. At last, though, there was another gust, the map flipped sideways and Polygnotus grabbed it.

'Put that in your pipe and smoke it,' Cassius growled.

Doris giggled again.

'What will he do with it, do you think?' she asked.

'Take it straight to Rome, I hope,' said Cassius. 'Or Parthia. Either way, he'll be gone for a while. Best of all, he thinks he has Antony's invasion plans, when in fact he has the complete opposite!"

'You're brilliant,' Doris sighed.

CHAPTER TWENTY-TWO
Bo's House.
The 21st Century

'You were right,' Bo told Cavendish. 'Doris wasn't poisoned or stabbed, but she did run into Polygnotus in the back streets of Alexandria. Which is almost as bad. I think Cassius may have got rid of him, though. He managed to give him information about Antony's plans for Parthia. False information, of course. With any luck, Polygnotus has gone scuttling off to Octavian with the wrong map! Cassius is very clever, don't you think?'

Cavendish licked a paw luxuriantly.

'Very clever,' he smiled. 'But what about Antony and Cleopatra? Did you see them playing pranks on people? Did they order tuna sandwiches from a street trader?'

'*Yesss,*' Bo replied cautiously.

'So you saw what good friends they were?'

'Yes, but I knew that already. Why did you want me to see it again?'

'Because whilst Antony was making plans to invade Parthia, the Parthians were having their own ideas. They began to move into Antony's eastern territories. That was bad news. When Antony heard about it he left Alexandria immediately, returned to Rome, and made a very shrewd move.'

'Which was?'

'He got married.'

'In Rome? To whom?'

'To Octavian's sister.'

'Oh, no!' gasped Bo. 'Cleopatra will be *furious*!'

Cavendish shook his head.

'No she won't. She knew it was illegal for Romans to marry foreigners. She knew she couldn't be Antony's wife herself, so why *not* let him marry Octavian's sister? That way, Antony could keep an eye on Octavian.'

"Keep your friends close, but your enemies closer',' Bo recited. 'My mother used to say that. It means that if you know what you're enemies are planning they'll be less able to take you by surprise. She told me I should always be friendly with Jack Russells, even if I didn't really mean it.'

'That was exactly Antony and Cleopatra's theory. It meant sacrifices, though. Antony was away for a long time. Whilst he was gone, Cleopatra had twins, a boy and a girl. They were Antony's children, but he didn't see them until they were five-years-old.'

'He was gone for five *years*?'

'More, from Alexandria. But Doris and Cleopatra saw him sooner than that. By then, Antony had driven the Parthians back from his territories, his reputation in Rome had soared and he'd become a hero again. He arranged to meet Cleopatra and Doris in Antioch, the capital of Syria, and from there they travelled together to a place called Zeugma.'

    'The Zeugma on Antony's map?'

    'Yes.'

    'The Zeugma on the way to Parthia?'

    'Yes.'

CHAPTER TWENTY-THREE
Zeugma, Syria.
May 36BC

Doris narrowed her eyes and looked across the Euphrates River, past groves of pistachio trees to the hazy hills of Mesopotamia.

'On the other side of those,' she whispered to herself, 'is Parthia.'

'Doris?' Menander called. 'Oh, there you are.'

He crouched down and put an arm around Doris's shoulders.

'Parthia is somewhere out there,' he said as he stroked her back. 'After all these years, Antony is on the brink of fulfilling Caesar's ambition. He has gathered the greatest army the world has ever seen, and you are a part of it.'

'Only until tomorrow,' Doris thought. 'Tomorrow you and I will set out for Alexandria, and Antony and Cleopatra will leave for Parthia without us.'

Doris had mixed feelings about this. She'd only just been reunited with Antony after three-and-a-half years. Now he was leaving her again, and this was to be their last night together for goodness knew *how* long.

Still, she'd got the better deal. She certainly didn't

want to go to Parthia. In Alexandria she'd be at home. She'd have Menander and all her lovely and familiar things. That had to be better than tramping across some vast, mysterious and unconquered land.

Menander patted her head.

'Come inside now,' he said. 'It's supper time.'

Doris trotted down the hall and into the dining room. It smelled wonderful. She jumped onto Antony's knee and gazed at the spread. *Most* of her favourite foods were there. The only thing missing was roasted dormouse, but that was all right. She'd have plenty of those when she got back to Demetrius in Alexandria. There were loads of other delicious things. Antony piled her plate with a selection of them, and she settled down contentedly to eat and listen to his last-minute plans.

Antony had always known that his only hope of beating the Parthians was to take them by surprise. But his army of seventy-thousand men and ten-thousand horses couldn't exactly be hidden. There was no way he could keep his preparations a secret, so he hadn't tried. He'd done the opposite.

'They'll think they know everything by now,' he said as he used his teeth to rip the flesh from a chicken leg. 'They'll have seen us. They'll be waiting for us. I dare say there's thousands of them on the other side of that river. They'll expect us to cross it, of course. That's the most direct route from here to their border. How *little* they know! We'll follow the river north, then head for

Armenia. The Armenian mountains will give us good cover. After that, we'll have to move swiftly. We'll cross the plains, and by the time the Parthians discover the truth, it'll be too late.'

Doris breathed a sigh of relief.

'Thank goodness Antony hasn't changed his mind,' she mumbled to herself. 'It's been a long time since Cassius stole that map and gave it to Polygnotus. We'd be in real trouble if Antony had decided to do what it says. But he hasn't. The map still shows what he *won't* do, not what he will.'

'Stealth is what's required,' Antony said, tucking into more chicken. 'Stealth and speed.'

Cleopatra raised her glass.

'To stealth and speed!' she toasted. 'And something else besides...'

Doris and Antony looked up.

'...a baby!' Cleopatra announced.

'*Another* baby?' Doris was amazed. 'But you've got three already. *Four*, counting me. Still, Antony seems pleased.'

Antony had scrambled to hug Cleopatra.

'This is good news,' he said, 'but it means you must return to Egypt with Doris and Menander.'

'I will do no such thing!' the queen replied. 'I am going to Parthia as planned.'

Antony shook his head.

'No. A Roman army is not the best company for someone in your condition,' he said patiently. 'You must go home.'

'But that would leave you all alone,' Cleopatra pouted, 'and forsaken by those who love you.'

'That's true,' Antony agreed as he returned to his seat. 'And now I wish we'd brought Cassius with us.'

'Then send for him,' suggested Cleopatra.

'No. There isn't enough time. We must move on. Anyway, Cassius can't keep up with the cavalry, and there's no point in taking him if he can't be by my side.'

He plucked a fig from the bowl in front of him, tore it open and sucked absentmindedly at its flesh.

Doris grimaced.

She hated figs.

'If I must go home,' Cleopatra said quietly, 'then I would like to do so with Doris. We have never been apart, you see. Not since she was a tiny puppy. I was in exile, then. She and I have been through everything together.'

'So? What's changed?' Antony asked. 'The two of you will go back to Alexandria together.'

'Not this time,' Cleopatra replied. 'I will have the comforts of home, so you must have the comfort of Doris. You will be glad of her company. Doris? You shall go to Parthia with Antony.'

CHAPTER TWENTY-FOUR
Bo's House.
The 21st Century

'Cleopatra wanted to send Doris to Parthia,' Bo gasped. 'Did that happen? Did Doris really go there?'

'Not quite.'

'Oh, that's good,' said Bo. 'What do you mean, "not quite"? She must have gone somewhere. Do you know where she went?'

'Yes.'

'But you're not going to tell me?'

'No. I think you should see it first-hand,' the spaniel replied. 'Though perhaps not *all* of it. Doris was away for months and months.'

'Then I'd like to go back to the day she realised her journey was over,' Bo said. 'The day she turned around and headed home. She'll remember the months and months, and I'll know what happened without having to do it.'

'That's hardly in the spirit of things, now is it? The whole point about time travel is being able to live the experience. It isn't just about knowing what happened. Anyone can find *that* out.'

'How?'

'Books. The Internet.'

'I can't read. Doris could, but I can't.'

'Then I'll teach you.'

'How long will it take?'

'Months, probably.'

'More months than Doris was away?'

'Maybe.'

'How will I find this book? The one that says what happened?'

'Go to the library.'

'They won't let me in.'

'Then look on line.'

'I don't know how to do that, Cavendish.'

'Well then. You'd better be Doris instead.'

CHAPTER TWENTY-FIVE
Zeugma, Syria.
May 36BC

Just after sunrise one misty morning, Antony wrapped Doris in his red woollen cloak and carried her out of the house at Zeugma.

A group of mounted cavalry officers were waiting on the road, and Antony's new horse, Ariadne, was standing patiently amongst them. Antony handed Doris to one of the officers, led Ariadne aside and sprang into her saddle. It was a skill that took years to perfect, and Antony was an expert. Roman saddles had no stirrups, but they did have a prong on each corner to stop the rider from falling off, so a man had to leap very high indeed to avoid a painful landing.

Antony turned Ariadne's head, pressed his calves against her sides and trotted her to the front of the group. Halfway there, he paused, whisked Doris from the officer's horse and settled her on his lap.

The march to Parthia had begun.

For the next four months, Antony's army did everything

in the same order, by the same manner and at the same time every day. At dawn, the lightly-armed scouts and archers set out. Their job was to reconnoitre the next stretch and look for possible trouble or ambush. After them went some of the more heavily-armed soldiers. They cleared the road ahead, sometimes literally if it involved chopping down a tree or moving a boulder, selected a place for that night's stopover and began to build a camp. Then came some of the cavalry, yet more soldiers and, about an eighth of the way down the line, Antony, Doris and their officers, who were backed up by the rest of the army, plus the heavy weapons, baggage and livestock.

Riding with Antony was the perfect way for Doris to see what was going on. Ariadne was an honest, sure-footed grey with sturdy legs and a reassuringly large bottom. She was also the ideal height for Doris, being low enough for Doris to jump from, but sufficiently tall to cover the ground at a good pace and give Doris a view. Best of all, she'd been trained to kneel down, as had most Roman cavalry horses, so Doris could remount her without any help.

Sometimes, Antony would turn Ariadne and they'd retrace their steps to visit and encourage those behind them. When that happened, Doris would stand on the front of the saddle and bark as the men cheered, raised their spears and reached to pat her. It was atmospheric and exciting, back there. There were marching feet, prancing hooves and clinking armour, and everything seemed more intense, be it the weather or the mood, rainy or hot, exultant or exhausted.

One day, Antony made Ariadne travel so far backwards that Doris began to think they might end up in Zeugma again, but finally, just after dark, they stopped.

They were surrounded by high silhouettes and twinkling lanterns. Doris thought the silhouettes were buildings, and that the tail-end of the army had camped in a village, which was just as well, because she wouldn't have slept if she'd known where she *really* was. It wasn't until the next morning, when the sun came up, that she realised she'd spent the night with the most feared and infamous section of the entire Roman army.

The heavy artillery.

The machines were still parked up and slumbering when Antony went to inspect them, but they didn't need to do anything for Doris to imagine what havoc they could cause. Their sheer size was enough. Doris trotted behind Antony as he strode past one massive machine after another, ran his hands over them and asked after their welfare. He treated them like giant pets, patting their legs affectionately, and even kissing some of them.

He reached a catapult as tall as a house.

'It shoots rocks, Doris,' he said proudly.

He'd spoken to her in Greek, but now switched seamlessly to Latin.

'Isn't that right?' he demanded of the catapult's

keeper.

'Yes, master,' the keeper replied.

'Well, then. Show us! Show Doris what it does! She's never seen a Roman catapult!'

The man gleefully explained how one end of the catapult's see-saw mechanism was pulled down as far as it would go and loaded with a slingful of rock. The end was then released again so it shot upwards in an arc until it hit the top of the frame with a bang and the sudden stop propelled the rock into the air.

'We have many types of catapult,' the man added as he ushered Antony and Doris past more weapons. 'Some can fire iron bolts, some specialise in darts or flaming torches. This one here...'

Next came a tour of the battering rams. Doris learned how the rams were set on carriages so they could be wheeled up to a city wall and swung backwards and forwards against it until it collapsed. The Roman legionaries would then charge over the resulting rubble and take the city by storm. The man omitted to mention the one thing that Doris already knew, which was that only good-looking women and children had any chance of surviving this onslaught. And that was only because they could be sold as slaves. Everyone else, including the dogs, would be slaughtered.

The man droned on and on and Doris stopped listening. She could have blamed it on the Latin and pretended she didn't understand him, but words like whizz, crush, squash, splat and dead weren't hard to translate. She knew what the man was saying and she was beginning to feel queasy.

She was saved by the trumpets.

They were sounding the order to pack up and move on. The soldiers rolled up their leather tents and harnessed the oxen to the artillery. Mules were brought up to the supply vehicles that carried bacon, grain, honey, oil, wine, weapons and parts. Horses were tacked, livestock herded, watchtowers dismantled. Everything of use would be packed and transported. Anything else would be burned. Nothing would be left behind.

Antony's army followed the Euphrates until the river had narrowed into an ice-cold, rushing stream in the mountains of Armenia. This was strange country for Doris. She was well-travelled, but she'd barely risen above sea level. Now she was in real mountains. There were craggy rocks, shaley paths and lush green valleys covered in thousands of delicate flowers. There were shadowy people, too. Gaggles of brightly clothed children appeared as if from nowhere, and the soldiers threw scraps for them. Most of the children rushed out, snatched the food and disappeared, but the braver ones lingered to stare and point before scampering away, shrieking with laughter.

Many of the birds were completely new to Doris, and there were plenty of small mammals, as well as wolves, bears, leopards and wild goats. The soldiers hunted some of these animals. The skins were scraped clean and used for warmth at night, and the meat was eaten to save the livestock for another day, though Doris did draw the line at wolf stew. Food on the road was simple but good. It had to be. The soldiers walked all day in heavy armour and carried their own weapons and tents.

The mountains tumbled into rolling hills and then flattened out completely. This was the Araxes River valley, and the place where Antony needed to pick up speed. Friendly Armenia would soon be behind him, and the open country to the south would leave his army exposed to attack. Crossing the plains at a snail's pace would be suicidal, but the heavy artillery was unable to do much else. The huge pieces of machinery were cumbersome and had to be dragged along. Stealth and speed were not their forte, so Antony decided to split his force in two. The slow-moving artillery and baggage trains would follow at their own pace, with five-thousand legionaries and thirteen-thousand Armenian soldiers to guard them, and Antony and Doris would charge ahead with the rest of the army.

CHAPTER TWENTY-SIX
Phraaspa, Media.
September 36BC

Antony pointed between Ariadne's ears.

'There it is, Doris,' he whispered. 'The city of Phraaspa. Self contained, heavily fortified and stuffed full of treasure! Perfect. We will take it over and use it as a base. From there, we will attack Parthia.'

Doris narrowed her eyes and peered ahead. Sure enough, something large and solid was rising out of the landscape.

She looked to her left. Ariadne was in the centre of a long line of cavalry. It had spanned the plain and was moving forward at a steady, relentless trot. Doris could see the horses' nostrils flaring and their forelocks curving back in the breeze. She could hear the creak of their tack and the clink of their riders' swords, but she could see nothing below their heads. So many horses ranged in a line had caused the dry earth to rise up in puffs. Now their chests and legs were enveloped in powdery dust, and their heads hovered in the air like disembodied phantoms.

Doris couldn't see the nine-thousand horses and fifty-five-thousand legionaries behind her, but she could hear them all right. They were so perfectly in step that they sounded like one giant beast.

She shuddered and turned to face Phraaspa.

'What must it be like in there?' she muttered to herself. 'Can they see us? They *must* be able to hear us. What are they thinking?'

'They'll have heard the stories,' said Antony from over her shoulder. 'They'll know what a Roman army can do. The very sight of us will be enough to make them surrender.'

Doris thought he was probably right about that.

He wasn't.

When the Romans reached the city and surrounded it, the Phraaspans barricaded themselves behind their sturdy walls and refused to give in. From the Romans' point of view, this was inconvenient but not a disaster. They could make short work of cutting the city off from the outside world. Nothing and no one would be able to enter it. Its people would face thirst, disease and starvation and, by the time the Roman artillery arrived, the citizens of Phraaspa would be so weak they'd surrender anyway.

Antony's army excavated a huge mound of earth and enclosed the city inside it. Then they built a comfortable camp for themselves and settled down to wait. Phraaspa was under siege.

Doris was still hoping its people would see sense.

The heavy artillery was due any day now. She'd heard enough of the boring mechanic's lecture to know exactly what *that* meant, and she didn't want to watch it.

Anyway, she was getting restless. In all her months on the road, she'd never spent more than a night in one place. She'd usually arrived at dusk and left at dawn, which gave no time to do anything except eat and sleep. On the rare occasions she'd encamped early, or left late, she'd had somewhere new to explore. Somewhere with interesting smells and unsuspecting wildlife for her to chase.

Phraaspa had been like that too, at first. But now the wildlife had left, or been eaten by the soldiers, the smells were stale, and she'd covered every inch of the camp twice over. She'd never thought she'd say it after four months of riding, but Doris was looking forward to getting back in the saddle and moving on.

One evening, when Antony was playing dice with his officers, Doris, who was sitting close by, heard the faintest rumble of hooves. The artillery and baggage were expected at any moment, so Doris jumped onto Antony's knee and pawed his hand.

'Ha! Doris,' he said, stroking her ears but continuing with his game. 'Don't do that. You're scratching me.'

Doris barked.

Antony glanced at her and then at the entrance to his tent.

'Something's up,' he called to the guards. 'Take a look outside. It could be the artillery and the...'

Before he'd finished speaking, the galloping hooves were audible to all, and Antony leapt to his feet, knocking over his stool and tipping Doris to the floor.

The horses skidded to a stop and their riders rushed into the tent. Doris could tell by their faces that the news was bad. They'd been expected to say that the baggage train and artillery were about to arrive. What they actually said was that the Parthians had ambushed it. The Armenian escort had run away, and Antony's five-thousand legionaries had been slaughtered. Then, since the Parthians had no idea how to use the heavy weapons and no need for the supplies, they'd set light to the lot.

Everything had been burnt to ashes. Antony had lost five-thousand men, his heavy weaponry, and all of the grain, food, tools, tack, tents, machinery parts and clothing from the baggage train.

It was a disaster.

Antony had thousands of men and horses to feed, and nothing with which to do it. He *had* to force the Phraaspans to surrender, preferably before they ate whatever food they had left.

So he waited.

And he waited.

And then the Parthians, fresh from wiping out his artillery and baggage trains, turned their attention to him.

CHAPTER TWENTY-SEVEN
Phraaspa, Media.
October 36BC

The Parthians fought on horseback.

Their mounted archers were wild and fearless. They wore no armour and little besides, and their ponies were small and wiry, fast as the wind and able to spin on a coin.

Doris had never seen, could never have imagined such fascinating people. She loved their amazing skill with bow and arrow, their nippy ponies, and the way they melted back into the landscape.

Yes, she was afraid of them, but she knew she was comparatively safe. If she stayed in Antony's tent, she could poke her nose through its front flaps and watch the archers tear down from the mountains. She'd hold her breath as they closed in, then breathe out with a long sigh when they suddenly turned away. Antony's men would chase after them, then, and the archers would turn again, equally suddenly, and attack. Or not. Sometimes they'd just keep riding until they disappeared. Doris knew she wasn't supposed to admire the enemy, but when it came to the Parthian archers, she just couldn't help herself.

She could watch them for hours.

Their fighting partners, the Parthian cavalry, were something else entirely. Of them, Doris was terrified. They wore sinister armour made from reticulated iron scales. It covered the men from head to toe, but most frightening of all, it covered their horses, too. The horses' heads were encased in iron masks and had matching blankets which reached to their knees. They and their dark riders were so well protected that they could make death-defying charges straight at the Roman soldiers. Their weapons weren't bows and arrows, but lances. Long, lethal lances that were expertly balanced and weighted, and so accurate that they could whizz through the air in a flash and cut clean through two men.

Doris had seen it happen.

The Parthian heavy cavalry were creepy in the extreme, like something from another world.

They gave Doris nightmares.

Day after day the arrows and lances rained down, and yet the Parthians never seemed to run out of them. Doris didn't understand how that could be, until she heard Antony and his officers talking about it.

The secret was camels. Hundreds of them. They were hidden in the hills, and their backs were bristling with weaponry. When a rider had fired his last shot, he simply turned his horse and headed for the camels. It was because of them that the Parthians could fight all day.

The Parthians were also totally unpredictable. They'd harass the Romans constantly, then disappear for a nerve-racking lull. Sometimes this lull lasted for a few hours, sometimes a whole day would pass before anything happened.

This unpredictability meant that Antony's soldiers could never relax and became increasingly frazzled. They were also growing weak from lack of food. When their morale was nearing rock-bottom, Antony began to negotiate with the King of Parthia. He said he would leave Phraaspa and take his army with him if the king would promise to call off his men. The king agreed, and the Romans prepared to decamp.

Doris stood up, shook the dust from her fur and padded over the hard-packed earth. She followed the rails of the corral, where a hundred or more cavalry horses were trotting in a continuous, restless circle. She passed a series of wooden pens where individual animals were being siphoned out of the herd and saddled up. She spotted Ariadne and barked hello, and Ariadne pawed the ground and whinnied in reply. It would take a long time, hours probably, but the day had come at last. Doris and Ariadne would soon be together again, riding home.

Doris reached Antony's tent and looked longingly at the mountains of Armenia.

'Tomorrow,' she muttered to herself. 'Tomorrow they'll be closer. Home will be closer. I'll see my mistress and her new baby. I'll see Menander and Charmion and Demetrius. He'll cook me roasted dormice and I'll eat them straight from his hand. I wonder if Cassius will be there? I hope so. I shall tell him all about Phraaspa, how much I've missed him and how lucky he was to be left behind.'

She turned to go into the tent, but as she did so she noticed something strange about the Armenian sky.

She'd never seen a sky that looked that way.

She'd never seen clouds that looked that way.

She shook her head bemusedly and pushed at the tent flap with her paw.

CHAPTER TWENTY-EIGHT
The Armenian border, Media.
November 36 BC

Antony's soldiers had been weak when they'd left Phraaspa, but they'd become weaker still on the road to Armenia. It had taken them a month to reach the border, and they'd done it on empty stomachs.

The King of Parthia had promised that his men would leave Antony and his troops alone.

They hadn't.

They'd kept up their ambushes all the way. They'd harried and teased the Romans, mowed them down with flat out charges or picked them off with individual arrows.

It was late afternoon, and the Romans had reached the Araxes River. All they had to do now was cross it, and they'd be back in Armenia. They knew the Parthians wouldn't follow. Most had already given up and gone home, and only one very persistent group was still hanging on. The light was fading and the river was too cold and fast to cross in the dark, so Antony had decided to set up camp and wait until morning.

Doris had been riding all day, and had just got down from Ariadne. She wanted to stretch her legs and began to follow some soldiers who'd gone to collect firewood.

She had her nose to the ground and was sniffing out a porcupine when it happened.

A hail of Parthian arrows rained down from a craggy outcrop, and Doris felt a sharp pain and a weird vibration. She turned, glanced back, and saw an arrow shaft sticking out of her shoulder. It was still quivering. She squealed, as much in surprise as pain, and then everything went black.

A centurion carried her to Antony's tent, laid her out on the bed and then left. She knew she wasn't alone. She could hear people whispering and kneeling beside her. Someone poured water over her head to bring her round, and she shook herself. The arrow shook, too, and she tried to catch it in her teeth just as Antony rushed in.

'No!' he scolded. 'Don't pull at it! You'll snap the shaft and leave the head. We must get it out in one.'

He crouched down, twisted on his haunches and called over his shoulder.

'Hurry up, man!' he said.

'Ready!' came the reply.

The centurion returned, pushed the tent flap aside and strode towards him.

Doris could see he was holding something behind his back. She caught a whiff of hot metal and suddenly realised what was about to happen. She'd seen arrowheads being removed from legionaries. Strong, fit, virile soldiers had been reduced to blubbing babies. They'd screamed blue

191

murder.

'No!' she yelped as she struggled to escape.

'Help me hold her!' shouted Antony.

'Yes, master,' said the centurion, and Doris felt the pressure of his hands on her back.

'We must do this, sweetheart,' Antony whispered. 'We must get the arrow out. It will take no more than a second. I promise.'

He reached out a hand.

'The knife,' he said.

Doris closed her eyes and felt Antony's arm shift against her and take the knife.

She knew it would be the sharpest in camp. She knew it had been heated over a fire to sterilize it. It was probably the sharpest, cleanest knife in the whole world.

She screamed.

'I can't do this,' Antony cried.

'Yes, you can,' the centurion replied. 'You did it only yesterday. Remember Oppius? He was screaming, too. You saved his life, master.

'Yes, but Oppius could tell me when to stop. He could *tell* me when he needed a break from the pain. Time to breathe. Doris can't do that. This arrow hasn't gone deep. It could work its own way out.'

'It could. It could also become infected. Doris may not be able to tell you when to stop, but neither can she tell you that her shoulder is throbbing, that she has a fever...'

'Then I'll watch her. I'll stay up all night if needs be.'

'And if the arrow doesn't work free? You'll still have to remove it. She may be too sick by then. Take it out, master. Take it out *now*, whilst she has the strength to endure it.'

'I can't,' Antony replied.

'Then I'll do it,' said the centurion. 'I'll do it, but you must hold her down.'

Doris felt Antony lift her onto his knee. She screamed and there was a quick, searing pain. She was still screaming when they bathed and bandaged her. It was only later, when she'd been given extra rations and a front row seat by the fire, and Antony was telling his soldiers about her operation, that she began to feel ashamed.

'The arrow must have hurt like hell when it first struck her,' he said. 'She was in shock and I don't mind admitting I was worried. I couldn't bring myself to remove the arrowhead myself. I didn't want to have to dig into her. But then, just before it *was* removed, I noticed it had hit a bony part of her body. Only its tip and sides had penetrated flesh. It could have worked its way out, but leaving it was too much of a risk. In the end the job was quick and easy. The arrow slipped out like a donkey's fart!'

He slapped his thigh and roared with laughter, the soldiers joined in, and Doris did her best to smile.

The following day, the army crossed the fast-flowing, icy waters of the Araxes River and, when everyone had reached the other side, a head count was taken.

The greatest army in the world had lost twenty-four-thousand men since leaving Zeugma. Many had been killed by the Parthians, but the biggest culprits were exhaustion and starvation. Those still alive were exhausted and starving, too, but at least they were in friendly Armenia. The Parthians were behind them, and the rest of the journey should be easy.

Back in Phraaspa, Doris had noticed something strange about the Armenian skies.

Now she learnt what it meant.

Snow.

She found it exciting at first. She'd never seen snow. She loved its soft flakes and the way they twinkled on her coat or landed on the ground and disappeared.

Then, one morning, she awoke to find that the flakes had settled, and there was a blanket of white outside her tent. She pranced about and then lay down and rolled, which was when she discovered that the snow wasn't just pretty, but also cold and wet.

After that, the snow just kept coming. It formed drifts so high that Doris could no longer walk in it. When she did, it froze into icy balls which clumped around her ankles and made her feet too heavy to lift. Worst of all, it sometimes arrived with bitter winds which turned the ends of her already damp fur into a frosty crust that crackled when she moved.

When these blizzards came, Doris couldn't see beyond her nose. She was unable to smell and too cold to feel, but she could still hear. Sometimes she wished she couldn't. She didn't like the sound of starving, exhausted soldiers crying through the squall. She wanted to block out their last breaths and the pathetic whinnies of their dying horses.

The winds could last for hours or days, then drop as suddenly as they'd begun. There'd be an eerie quiet, then, and the men would regroup and trudge out to anyone who'd stumbled. They couldn't venture too far. The blizzards might return at any moment. The soldiers prodded any bodies they found to see if they were dead or merely sleeping, in which case they'd lift them to their feet and slap them awake. Falling asleep in the snow could be fatal. If they found a dead man, they left him where he lay, with his frozen arms outstretched, but dead horses were butchered. They were jointed on the spot and their meat, still glittering with frost, was carried back to the fires.

Doris's worst fear was that Ariadne might die and Doris would unwittingly eat her. The horse's round bottom had wasted away, her hip and shoulder bones were sticking out and Doris could count her ribs. Antony no longer rode her all day. Whenever possible, he packed the hollow in his saddle with a bearskin, put Doris on top, and led Ariadne by the reins. Doris wished she could speak the secret language that horses and dogs shared. She'd never heard of such a thing, but she was sure it must exist. Cats and dogs had a shared language, Felcanish, so why wouldn't horses and dogs have one too? They'd been friends of man for centuries, after all. They were working partners, whereas cats did nothing but lie around, sleep and eat. Whatever the answer, Doris

didn't know it, and since Ariadne didn't seem to know it either, they communicated as best they could by nuzzling each other, stamping their feet and shaking their heads and tails.

The horsemeat saved a lot of lives, but there wasn't enough of it and there was nothing else to eat. When there was some horse, Antony was always last to be served. He even fed Doris before he fed himself. They sat with the men, all huddled together under blankets and shields, and everyone ate their meagre rations. Antony would bury Doris deep in his clothing, pull a bearskin over her head and pass tit-bits to her. They were mostly gristle and bone, but they were warm, and Doris sucked on them gratefully. She was miserable and thin, but also strangely happy. The arrow wound had healed into a satisfactory scab and, though she was facing hardship for the first time in her life, she was being as tough and strong and brave as she possibly could be.

Even the centurions were proud of her.

CHAPTER TWENTY-NINE
Luece Come, Syria.
February 35 BC

Doris's scab was itching. She contorted herself into a ball and tried desperately to nibble at it, but she just couldn't reach the spot.

'Leave it,' said Antony crossly.

Doris slumped onto the sand and put her chin on her paws. Then she got up again and went to sit on the shoreline.

'You'll get a scar,' Antony called after her more kindly. 'We don't want that now, do we?'

Doris didn't really care whether she got a scar or not. She knew she was lucky to be alive, out of the snow and sitting on a beach. Phraaspa and Armenia were far behind her and she was back in familiar territory. Yet the last few weeks had been some of the most miserable of her life.

Antony had sat for days on end saying nothing, not even to her. He'd just stared blankly into space.

Doris had tried to cheer him up, but she'd soon realised there wasn't much she could do, other than stay close to him and hope he'd feel better soon. She knew he'd done his best. For every minute of the horrific retreat from Phraaspa, he'd thought of his men and put them first. He'd had no airs and graces and had expected no special treatment for himself. He'd supported the weak, spoken to the dying and saved many lives. Yet in spite of his leadership and kindness, another eight-thousand soldiers had died in the snow.

When the ragged army had finally stumbled back into Syria, it had been half its original size.

Things should have got better when news came that Cleopatra was on her way with ships full of food and money for the soldiers. But the news had meant another wait, and now Doris and Antony had been here for weeks, with nothing to do but watch the horizon.

Doris stood up, shook the sand from her fur and padded back to Antony. He hadn't moved. He was exactly where she'd left him, still gazing out to sea, still searching for Cleopatra's ships.

Doris lay down beside him and put her head in his lap as he reached out and stroked her scab.

'We'll put some olive oil on that tonight,' he said. 'See if we can't soften it a bit. It's the tightness that makes it itch. You mustn't be left with a scar, Doris. I could do without that. I've got too much to explain to your mistress as it is.'

CHAPTER THIRTY
Bo's House.
The 21st Century

'Dreadful,' said Bo. 'It's all dreadful. Antony and Doris are back in Syria now. They're safe, but Antony's lost over thirty-thousand men. He's miserable and he doesn't deserve it. He's a wonderful soldier, his men really love him and he's worked *so* hard to look after them all.'

'He's had terrible luck,' Cavendish agreed. 'If he hadn't lost the artillery and baggage trains he could have taken Phraaspa. He might even have made it to Parthia. He wouldn't have had to retreat through the snow...'

'I bet Octavian had fun,' said Bo bitterly. 'I bet he loved it. He must have had a field day, spreading the news that Antony had failed, how he'd turned back. How all those soldiers had died.'

'Oh, he had fun all right,' Cavendish replied.

'I *knew* it!'

'Octavian spread the news far and wide. He told everyone that Antony had had a fabulous victory, that he'd taken Phraaspa and conquered Media.'

'Wha...? Why? Why would he do that?'

'Because Media was incredibly wealthy.'

'Antony said that. He said Phraaspa was stuffed with treasure.'

Cavendish nodded.

'It was. And if people believed that Antony had captured all that treasure, then they'd also believe he didn't need help from Octavian. Which meant that Octavian could break all the promises he'd made.'

'Promises?'

'Many promises. Promises of extra soldiers, of money to pay them, and of land in Italy for them to retire to. Octavian had promised Antony all sorts of things.'

'I know about the soldiers,' Bo said. 'They were a swap for ships. Antony sent the ships, but I don't think the soldiers ever arrived.'

'Oh they arrived all right,' said Cavendish, 'but only in typical Octavian style.'

CHAPTER THIRTY-ONE
Luece Come, Syria.
Spring 35 BC

The sun was shining, the sand was warm and dry between Doris's toes, and the cavalry horses were grazing the flowery cliffs. Doris could see Ariadne's white coat gleaming amongst them. The horse had already put on weight, and Antony had begun to take her for gentle rides to rebuild her muscles. It was hard to believe she was the same creature who'd staggered here, half dead and starving, just a few weeks ago.

Spring had arrived, and so had Cleopatra.

The queen had brought Egyptian money to pay Antony's soldiers and Egyptian grain to feed them. Now her newly emptied ships were sitting high on the water and bobbing in the bay. Doris thought they'd be going home soon, and that she'd be going with them, but she couldn't be sure.

She couldn't be sure of anything, anymore.

She stood up and pottered back towards the house, but before she'd even reached the front door, she heard Antony shouting furiously and banging his fist on something hard.

She paused.

He rarely got cross with *her*, and never like this. Just to be sure, though, she quickly ran through the day's events.

'I *did* sleep on his favourite cloak last night,' she remembered, 'but then I often do that. I *may* have chewed his sandals, and I *know* I ate part of his lunch, but the sandals were old and the lunch was handed to me on a plate. So whatever Antony is ranting about, it's nothing to do with me. I hope.'

There was a thump and a crack and a sound of splintering wood and breaking glass.

'And now he's smashing up the furniture.'

She followed the noise down the hall and into Antony's office. A chair with a snapped rail was lying upturned, and the floor was strewn with pieces of broken glass. Antony was holding a letter, and Cleopatra was kneading his shoulders with her thumbs.

'Well what did you expect?' the queen asked soothingly.

'EXPECT?' Antony roared. 'I *expect* a little *respect*!'

Doris heard familiar footsteps, and Charmion entered the room with a tray of wine, water and olives.

'Thank you, Charmion,' said Cleopatra. 'On the table, please. Then you may go.'

Charmion laid down her tray and hesitated.

'There's glass on the floor, mistress. Should I sweep it up? Doris might cut herself...'

'No!' Antony snapped. 'Leave it be!'

'Come here, Doris,' Cleopatra urged.

She picked Doris up and Charmion left and tactfully closed the door behind her.

'Now,' said Cleopatra as she poured Antony some wine and a dash of water, 'sit down and drink this.'

Antony huffed.

'Don't fuss, woman.'

He waved the letter in the air.

'It was a fussing woman got me into this mess in the first place!' he exclaimed as he stabbed at the letter with a forefinger.

'Yes. But from what I know of her, I doubt she'd be pouring you wine,' Cleopatra noted coolly. 'So sit down, calm down, and tell me again what you agreed with Octavian.'

Antony did as he was told. When he'd drunk the wine, he took a deep breath and hauled Doris onto his lap.

'It was two years ago, now,' he began. 'Octavian needed more ships in the west, and I needed more legionaries in the east. So I agreed to send him one-hundred and twenty ships...'

'Two squadrons.'

Antony nodded.

'He was supposed to send me twenty-thousand men in return.'

'Four legions.'

'There's no need to translate,' Antony said brusquely. 'I *do* know what squadrons and legions are.'

'Of course you do, darling. I'm just trying to get it all

clear in my *own* mind. Go on.'

'I sent the ships immediately, but I never received the men,' said Antony. 'Then this morning I get this!'

He smashed his fist against the letter.

'From your *wife*,' Cleopatra confirmed.

Doris sat up sharply.

'This should be good,' she thought. 'This should be *very* good.'

Doris had never met Antony's wife, but the lady was rumoured to be very beautiful, very intelligent and a little old-fashioned. She was also Octavian's sister. So not exactly Cleopatra's best friend.

'My *wife*,' said Antony, 'is currently on her way to Athens. She writes to say that she is bringing the soldiers her brother promised me. She clearly believes I will be pleased to hear that they number...'

He flung the letter into the air.

'I can't even tell you what they number,' he growled. 'It's an *insult*!'

Cleopatra retrieved the letter, read it, then handed it back to Antony.

'Octavian has sent you two-thousand soldiers, plus some food and supplies,' she said. 'He is also returning seventy of the ships you lent him.'

'Pah!' Antony barked. 'The man's supposed to be clever, yet he can't even add up. He owes me ten *times* that many soldiers. And what am I supposed to do with seventy war-torn, unmanned ships? It's soldiers I need, and it's soldiers I am due!'

Cleopatra paced the floor.

'We must think about Octavian's offer,' she muttered pensively. 'It is clearly a deliberate insult, but you must respond to it with care.'

Doris fancied she could hear her mistress's brain whirring.

'Accept the ships and men,' said Cleopatra suddenly. 'Reply to your wife and say she must send the troops and ships, but return herself to Rome.'

'You're right,' Antony agreed. 'That's what I'll do. Meanwhile,' he added as he picked up a scroll, 'I hope this brings better news. I see by the hand that it might.'

He slid his thumb under the scroll's seal and stretched the paper open.

'Yes!' he exclaimed.

He turned to Doris.

'This letter is from a friend of mine, Publius Propertius. He says that he will arrive here soon and that he is bringing Cassius with him! We can all go back to Alexandria together. Shall we take Ariadne, too?'

Doris wagged her tail.

CHAPTER THIRTY-TWO

Bo's House.
The 21st Century

'I see what you meant, now,' Bo told Cavendish. 'Octavian sent only a tenth of the soldiers he owed to Antony. Antony's wife was with them, but Antony sent her back to Rome without even asking to see her.'

'She was nothing but a pawn in Octavian's game,' said Cavendish. 'She loved Antony and wanted the best for him, but she was far too innocent. She had no clue that the soldiers were a tenth of the number due. She just couldn't see how manipulative her brother was. She wasn't good at mind games, and neither was Antony. He played straight into Octavian's hands and gave him exactly what he wanted. Octavian gleefully told everyone that his sister had been insulted and that Antony was a weak man who'd fallen under Cleopatra's spell.'

'Octavian was such a *schemer*!'

Cavendish nodded.

'He was determined to turn the Romans against Antony.'

'Not possible,' said Bo, 'the Romans worshipped Antony.'

'The Roman *soldiers* did, but Antony hadn't set foot in Rome for four years. He'd given Octavian the upper hand when it came to gossip. He should probably have gone back to Rome and stopped the rot, but something happened. Something so lucky that Antony couldn't resist making the most of it.'

Bo jumped up and down.

'What?' she asked. 'What happened?'

'The King of Media had a serious argument with The King of Parthia. It was so serious that the Medians promised Antony that if he tried to invade Parthia again, they would help him.'

'Wow!'

'Wow, indeed. But there's more. Antony went back to Armenia, captured its king, stole its treasure, and put his own men in charge. The road to Parthia was wide open and Antony was a hero again.'

CHAPTER THIRTY-THREE
The Gymnasium, Alexandria, Egypt.
Autumn, 34BC

Doris had been home for eighteen months. She'd never forget the horrors of Armenia, but she was almost back to her old self. True, she felt the cold more than she once had, and her shoulder sometimes stiffened up where the arrow had hit it but, as Menander had pointed out, she *was* getting on in years.

Antony was *completely* back to his old self. He hadn't forgotten Armenia, either. He'd learnt many lessons there, and he and Cleopatra had been working hard to make the most of them. They were going to have another shot at invading Parthia.

The first steps had already been taken. Antony had returned to Armenia, captured its king, stolen its treasure, and left his own men in charge. Better still, The King of Media had argued with The King of Parthia and was now promising to support Antony. The road to Parthia was beckoning, Antony was riding high, and a huge crowd had gathered in the Gymnasium to congratulate him.

The Gymnasium was one of the largest and grandest

buildings in the whole of the Mediterranean, and it was packed full of people. They were staring up at a high, terraced platform. It was made of silver and surrounded by a mass of body guards with washboard stomachs, tough faces and biceps as fat as marrows.

On the platform's top level, seated side by side on golden thrones, were Antony and Cleopatra. Cleopatra was sporting her fabulous costume of the goddess Isis, Antony was dressed as the god Dionysus. One step below them were four more thrones, one for each of Cleopatra's children, and below that, lying across a pile of zebra skins, were Doris and Cassius.

Doris rolled onto her back and yawned.

'Sit up straight and behave yourself,' Cassius snarled. 'You're on display.'

'But we've been here for *hours*, Cassius. And anyway, you're not sitting up, so why should I?'

'Because I'm a lion and I look my best lying down. Let's play a game. Why don't you describe the children to me, tell me what they're wearing?'

'You *know* what they're wearing.'

'Do it anyway. It'll keep us both amused. Better still, you'll have to sit up.'

'Oh, all right.'

Doris flipped onto her front and sat up.

'I'll start with Ptolemy Philadelphus,' she said.

This was the baby of the family, the one Cleopatra had announced was on its way just as she was about to leave for Parthia with Antony. He'd been born whilst Antony and Doris were waiting for Phraaspa to surrender, and was now two-years-old and making his first public appearance.

'There's a silk bonnet on his head,' Doris described. 'On top of that is a jewelled coronet. He has a little white jacket and trousers, and a miniature purple cloak with matching booties.'

'Good. Next?'

'The twins,' Doris replied. 'Alexander Helios and Cleopatra Selene. They look very exotic, especially Alexander. His coat is long and smothered in embroidery and it has wide sleeves. He's wearing a tall hat. It's wrapped in a white turban with a splay of peacock feathers on the front.'

'Caesarion?'

'Ah, lovely Caesarion,' Doris sighed. 'Caesarion looks beautiful.'

She wasn't being biased, she loved all the children equally, but Cleopatra's son by Julius Caesar really *did* look beautiful. He was a teenager, now, and was thought by all who knew him to be handsome and charming.

'He's sitting slightly in front the others,' Doris continued. 'His outfit is made from rose pink silk. He has a bunch of hyacinths fastened to his shoulder and a belt of amethyst and sapphire. His shoes are dotted with tiny pink pearls and fastened with white ribbons. He looks just like a miniature king.'

'He's supposed to,' said Cassius. 'They all are. Don't look so puzzled, Doris. Antony's about to make a speech. All will become clear.'

'As Nile mud,' Doris scoffed.

Antony rose to his feet and the crowd erupted into a frenzy of cheers and chants in Egyptian, Greek and Hebrew. He listened in appreciation for several moments, then raised his hand for silence and began to unravel a papyrus scroll. He held the base of the scroll against his hip, stretched the paper out in front of him and began to read.

'Whatsoever I propose herewith, I do in honour of Julius Caesar and of his legitimate son, Caesarion...'

'Ouch!' Cassius winced. 'That was aimed straight at Octavian. He won't like it, and neither will the snobs of Rome. They prefer to forget about Caesar's dalliance with Cleopatra.'

'It wasn't a dalliance,' Doris protested, 'they loved each other.'

Cassius shook his mane.

'It doesn't matter. The Romans don't expect their leaders to have children with wicked eastern queens.'

'Don't call her wicked. She's my ma and I love her and she's not wicked. She's not even eastern.'

'I know all that. I love her, too. I'm just saying that there are many who don't. Your mistress has enemies, Doris. You need to realise that. And top of the pile is one who is extremely powerful, clever and devious, namely Octavian.'

Doris swallowed hard and Antony continued with his announcement.

'I declare my son, Alexander Helios, to be King of Armenia, also overlord of Media and all territories east of the Euphrates as far as India...'

'Hold on a minute,' Doris whispered. "All territories east of the Euphrates as far as India'?' Doesn't that include Parthia?'

'Yes.'

'Can he do that?'

'Apparently.'

Antony's speech went on and on. He recited a stream of kingships, lordships, titles and lands, all of which he bestowed on his children. And then, having made his own children into two kings and a queen, Antony declared that Caesar's son, Caesarion, was to be king of them all, a King of Kings.

By the time the ceremony ended, Doris was hot, bothered and totally confused.

'Let's get some fresh air,' she told Cassius when they got back to the palace. 'I need you to tell me what all that was about. There must be more to it than riling Octavian and the snobs of Rome.'

'I don't think Antony *wants* to rile Octavian,' said Cassius as he and Doris reached the gardens. 'That's just a by-product. Antony has a long-term plan and it's a clever one. Making the children into kings and overlords may *sound* grand, but most of the countries he mentioned are Roman territories. The *real* power will remain with their *real* kings. He knows they can run their countries much better than any Roman. He really understands them, and their people.'

'Octavian still won't like it,' Doris tutted.

'No. He won't. But Antony has a good chance of

213

defeating Parthia now. If he does that, he'll be invincible and no one will care *what* Octavian thinks.'

'Do you really think Antony will try to conquer Parthia?'

'*Ohhh*, yes,' Cassius growled. 'It was Caesar's greatest ambition, and now it's Antony's. He and Cleopatra have worked hard. They've built a whole new fleet of support ships and Antony has rebuilt his army. They have Armenia and the support of Media. They won't give up now.'

'Then Ariadne and I shall have to hide somewhere. You'll have to feed us in secret every day until Antony's gone. I'm not going through that again and I don't want Ariadne to go through it either. Not even for Antony. Not for all the spices in India. Not for anything.'

CHAPTER THIRTY-FOUR

Bo's House.
The 21st Century

'Antony continued with his plans for Parthia,' said Cavendish. 'He returned to Armenia and set up camp on the Median border.'

'The Araxes River?' Bo shivered. 'I remember it well. I shan't go back there, Cavendish, so please don't ask.'

Cavendish shook his head.

'I don't have to,' he said. 'Doris didn't go. Antony left her and Ariadne in Alexandria. Though as it happens, I don't think they'd have minded being with Antony. He wasn't there for very long.'

'He didn't invade Parthia?'

'He couldn't. The quarrel between him and Octavian had been getting steadily worse. Word spread that Octavian was building ships, ready for some real fighting. When Antony heard the news, he left Armenia and headed west. Cleopatra had already built a massive fleet of ships to support the Parthian invasion. Now she packed those ships with money, arms and grain and sailed across the Mediterranean to meet with Antony.'

'Did she take Doris?'

'Yes.'

'What about Cassius?'

'Yes.'

'And Ariadne?'

'No. Ariadne was retired by then. She stayed behind.'

CHAPTER THIRTY-FIVE
Ephesus, Western Roman Asia.
May 32BC

The first time Doris rode the elephant, it made her feel sick.

It was supposed to be a treat.

She'd met the elephant's owner, King Mithridates of Commagene, at a dinner party. The king had taken a liking to her and invited her to join him for a short ride on the following day. The invitation could not be refused, since that would have been seen as an insult to the king. But then so, most probably, would throwing up on his knee. Doris had spent the whole, stomach-churning experience staring straight ahead, watching the horizon and swallowing hard.

The only time she'd ever been high up whilst moving at the same time was on the back of a horse.

Completely different.

The elephant was more than twice the height of even the tallest horse. It swayed. For every step it took, its body seemed to move the same distance sideways. It didn't make jolly clip-clop noises. It took silent, spongy steps and barely lifted its feet. Yet it could cover the ground at amazing speed, especially if frightened. There was no warning. It didn't snort, whicker or whinny. It just broke into a trot, threw its trunk in the air and trumpeted. Even more disconcerting was the way it flapped its ears. Doris judged other animals' moods by their ears. Forward was good. Back was bad. Backwards and forwards at the same time was both meaningless and worrying.

The strangest thing of all about riding the elephant was having to sit behind the man in charge. On a horse, Doris sat at the front, where she could see the very important ears, the rider's hands, the reins and, if she leant outwards, the horse's eyes.

On the elephant, Doris's seat was much further back, at the highest part of the elephant's spine. She sat on a throne with a safety rail around it and a canopy on top, for shade. The driver sat below her line of sight, astride the animal's neck. He used his feet and voice to control the beast, and occasionally thumped it on the back of its skull with an iron rod.

When it came to riding elephants, Doris had had a great deal to get used to, but after several days of enforced practice, she'd begun to like it.

It was then that the king had given Doris the elephant on permanent loan. Now it arrived every morning to collect her from the house where she and Cleopatra were staying. The canopied throne would already be in place, and the elephant would be decorated with fringes and jewels. When Doris was ready to board, it would sit on its bottom, just like a dog, then tip forward and tuck its forelegs under its chest until it was lying down.

A set of silver steps would then be propped against its side, Doris and Menander would take their seats on the throne, and the elephant would stand up again, giving Doris the best possible view of the great city of Ephesus.

She could see for miles around.

And there was a lot to see.

The city was an important trading post. It had been built at about the same time as Alexandria, and was essentially Greek in style, with wide streets laid out on a grid system. It faced the Aegean Sea, towards Athens, and had a natural harbour and good roads from the east.

In the past six months, these roads had been travelled by many eastern kings, including Mithridates, owner of the elephant. The kings had come to support Antony and Cleopatra in their fight against Octavian, and had brought entourages, advisors and thousands of soldiers and horsemen. The city was swirling with colourful characters and exotic costumes.

From her seat on the elephant's back, Doris could pick out vivid turbans, tight, wrinkly trousers and flared coats. There were tall hats, wide sleeves and jewelled belts; high collars, long beards and pointed shoes; soft boots laced with ribbon, and tunics studded with lozenges of gold. Some of the visitors were carried in litters, others rode high-stepping, long-maned Arab horses with arched necks and dished faces, still more sat in chariots drawn by camels.

220

When the elephant's sides brushed against the city walls, Doris would stand on her hind legs and look further afield.

Then she could see the vast Temple of Artemis, known as the most beautiful building in the world and, to the northwest, the harbour.

The harbour was stuffed full of ships. Doris could never have imagined that so many ships even existed, let alone that they could all be together in the same place at the same time. The tiny local fishing boats were crowded out and crushed for space by the biggest naval force since the days of Alexander the Great. Antony and Cleopatra's fleet boasted three-hundred troop carriers and five-hundred fighting ships, some built in Egypt, others on the nearby island of Cos.

Alongside the harbour, a new town had grown up. Doris had visited this town with Antony. It was where his army lived and slept, and it had offices, kitchens, fresh running water, lavatories, horse corrals and thousands of leather tents.

The elephant always took Doris home in time for lunch, after which she and Cassius would lie on the terrace and take a siesta.

One afternoon, when the lunch went on for an inordinately long time, Doris and Cassius left the table and went outside to doze beneath the dining room shutters. These were closed to keep out the afternoon heat, but since Antony and Cleopatra were still on the other side of them, Doris was doing her best to eavesdrop

221

on their conversation.

'I can't hear them very well,' she whispered to Cassius. 'Their voices are muffled by the shutters, but I think they're about to have a row.'

'So what's new?' came the lion's sleepy reply. 'They like a good row. It never lasts long.'

Doris huffed.

'You men are all the same. You're never interested in gossip.'

She strained her ears and picked up Antony's voice.

'The war hasn't even begun,' he grumbled. 'Yet already I'm being fired at from all sides. Every day, I'm bombarded by conflicting advice. Some say I could be in Italy by now. If only you'd agreed to return to Egypt, I could have invaded Italy at the end of winter and put a stop to this nonsense.'

'*What*? You know that's not true!' Cleopatra shouted. 'I won't have you say that, Antony. It was you who decided not to go to Italy. You said the southern Italian ports were too hard to capture!'

'I also said that I could not expect a welcome in my own country if you were with me.'

'Oh, I see. So you're happy to use my ships to get you there, but I'm not good enough to go too.'

'You're deliberately twisting things, and you know it! Ye gods, it's hot in here...'

'Open the shutters, then,' Doris implored. 'There's a nice breeze out here.'

Antony's footsteps crossed the dining room and Doris heard his fingers fiddle with the shutters' latch.

'Thank you, Isis!'

'Great,' Cassius growled. 'No chance of a nap now,' he yawned. 'I may as well join you.'

Antony pushed the shutters wide, then leant out of the window to hook them back against the villa's walls.

'Oh, hello you two,' he said. 'The truth is I probably couldn't have taken those ports,' he conceded as he returned to Cleopatra.

'Thank you,' the queen replied.

'It was all too much of a risk, with or without you. Octavian and I must come to blows. We all know that. But there is still the question of whether you should come any further with me. I must leave for Greece soon. If I take you, and Octavian's soldiers get to hear about it, then they might fight for him when they'd really rather fight for me.'

'Yes,' Cleopatra replied quietly. 'They might.'

'Did I hear what I think I heard?' Cassius asked. 'Is she admitting she's the problem?'

'She's not the *only* problem,' said Doris. 'It works both ways.'

'Yet it works both ways,' the queen mused.

'See!'

'My sailors will fight for me,' Cleopatra continued, 'for our alliance with the east and for freedom from Octavian. But they will *not* fight for you. If I do not go with you to Greece, my sailors' resolve may weaken. The same applies to the eastern kings and their troops. They might all retreat at the first sign of trouble.'

'Canidius Crassus would agree with you,' said

Antony. 'He says exactly that.'

Canidius Crassus was one of Antony's most important and trusted generals. He'd been at Phraaspa with Antony and Doris, and had also helped Antony with his recent conquest of Armenia. He'd always admired Cleopatra and thought that, when it came to politics, she was as good as any man.

'Canidius believes that since you have paid for most of my army and contributed so many ships and so much grain...'

'*And* helped you rally the eastern monarchs...' Cleopatra interjected.

'Yes, all right, that, too,' Antony laughed. 'Because of that, Canidius thinks you should stay by my side. And yet I still don't know what to do. What should I do? I've tried to make a decision. I've been to the temple, to the soothsayers, to the donkey-man...'

'The *donkey*-man?' Cleopatra repeated.

'Yes. The donkey-man. They say he can read the stars, which is about as unbiased an opinion as I'm likely to get around here.'

'Certainly less biased than that of some of your advisors,' Cleopatra agreed. 'They hate me.'

'Ah,' sighed Cassius, 'they're back to *that* again.'

'They don't *hate* you,' Antony groaned. 'They're *Romans*.'

'Exactly my point!' snapped the queen.

'I mean they know what people are saying in Rome...'

'So do I. Octavian portrays me as a wicked eastern

queen and conveniently forgets that I am of Greek descent...'

'Your descent doesn't matter to Octavian, woman! If anything, it makes things worse. Can't you see that? The Romans are paranoid and superstitious. Ancient prophesies say that the east and the Greeks will take them over. Can't you see how you play on their fear?'

There was a pause, and Doris heard the babble of liquid being poured, then the soft thump of a wine flask on wood followed by silence.

'Hippos! I can't hear a thing. What's happening? Why's it gone so quiet?'

'Why do you think?' Cassius groaned. 'They're making up, of course.'

'Let me stay, darling,' said Cleopatra eventually. 'In a few days time we will sail to Greece together. We will take a great army and an even greater navy. So what if Octavian declares war? Let him do that! We are more than ready for it.'

CHAPTER THIRTY-SIX

Bo's House.
The 21st Century

'Antony and Cleopatra had a fabulous army, brilliant Greek and Egyptian sailors, and plenty of money,' said Cavendish. 'When they reached Greece, they established bases all the way down its western coast and settled down to wait.'

'Again? For what?'

'For Octavian to declare war.'

'Why couldn't Antony do that? Everyone knew it was going to happen. Why not just get on with it?'

'Because Antony didn't want to be the one to start it. If he declared war on Octavian, it would be Rome against Rome. That's civil war, Bo, and the Romans had had far too much of that over the years.'

'So why was it different for Octavian?'

'It wasn't. Added to which, Octavian knew that the Roman soldiers would never fight against Antony. He was their hero.'

Bo wrinkled her nose and batted her ears with her paws.

'I don't understand,' she said. 'Are you telling me

they both did nothing?'

'For a while. Then Octavian took a solemn walk through the centre of Rome. It was winter by then and he was carrying a spear soaked in blood.'

'Whose blood?'

'Some poor beast. He'd sacrificed it in some ancient mumbo-jumbo Roman rite. It was so ancient that nobody did it any more, but it was very theatrical. Right up Octavian's street.'

'What did it mean?'

'It was a declaration of war. Octavian declared war, at last. But he did it with a twist. He was far too clever to go for Antony, so he decided to declare war on Cleopatra instead.'

'Cleopatra? Octavian declared war on Cleopatra?' Bo's small voice was panicky. 'Winter? He can't do anything in winter, can he? I know about winter, remember. No one can fight in winter.'

'That was Armenia, Bo,' said Cavendish. 'The weather in Greece is rather different. But you're right. Winter is not a good time for battles. So, yet again, there was a wait. Antony hunkered his soldiers down in cosy camps and moved his ships away from the blustery coast, into the shelter of the Ambracian Gulf. Still everybody waited.'

Bo suddenly felt dizzy.

She shook her head.

'What's the matter?' Cavendish asked.

'I don't know. Maybe it's the waiting. I can't bear the waiting. Do you remember the night we first met? The night of the thunderstorm?'

'Of course I...'

Bo raised a paw.

'The storm itself wasn't that bad,' she continued. 'It was only a storm. The worst thing was the anticipation. All those distant rumbles, the yellow sky. I knew what was coming and I just wanted to get it over with. I couldn't bear the waiting. I still can't. Storms always get me, but waiting for them is worse.'

She stood up and paced the floor.

'Doris is the same. She had all that waiting at Phraaspa, first for the city to surrender, then for the artillery to arrive. When it didn't, she had to wait again for Phraaspa to surrender. Then came the Parthian attacks, and still she was waiting, always wondering when they'd come, how bad it would be. Even when she reached Armenia, she was either waiting for the blizzards, or for the terrible calm that came after them.'

'Do you think she felt like that when she was in Greece?' Cavendish asked. 'Waiting for the war to begin?'

'I *know* she did. Cassius did, too. They hated the wait. But it was more than that. They, *we* felt the storm coming, everyone did. But we felt something else, too. We couldn't tell Antony about it. We had no words, you see. We couldn't warn him...'

Bo was panting.

She stumbled and fell. Her whole body was trembling.

Her legs were galloping but going nowhere, and her

228

lower jaw was working up and down in silent barks.

'Come back!' Cavendish barked. 'Come back to me! You are Bo, not Doris. Come back to me! Bo? Come back to the coal hole!'

Then Cavendish did something most extraordinary. Rather than comfort his distressed friend, he stepped away from her and sat down. He raised his head towards the coal hole's glass ceiling and, in a low, gravelly voice, recited aloud a short prayer to the goddess Isis. He spoke in Felcanish, the language which cats and dogs share, and the version he used was ancient.

As ancient as the days of Cleopatra.

'Great Goddess Isis Of The Moon,
Who from her mighty golden throne
Scatters diamonds in the sky.

Now look upon this precious soul,
Companion when you ruled the Nile
As mortal Cleopatra.

Send Doris Of The Lovely Hair
To be again the poodle Bo
In this, her given lifetime.

O Mother Of Nature And All That Breathes,
Bestow your blessings on us both.
Return my friend to me.'

When he'd finished his prayer, Cavendish laid a paw gently on Bo's head. She was already much calmer and had stopped shaking and turned on her side.

'Wake up, Bo,' the spaniel whispered. 'You're home. You're in the coal hole with Cavendish.'

Bo opened her eyes.

'What happened?' she asked.

'You got upset,' Cavendish replied. 'We were talking about Greece and you remembered something upsetting.'

'What? What did I remember?'

'I don't know,' said Cavendish.

Bo narrowed her eyes.

'Yes, you do,' she said. 'You know *exactly* what it was.'

CHAPTER THIRTY-SEVEN
Two weeks later

Cavendish had put the subject of Doris off limits.

'You've had too much of her,' he'd told Bo. 'You need a rest. You should concentrate on being yourself for a while. Enjoy your naps on the sofa. Go for walks, chase squirrels in the park and let small children pat you. Watch breakfast TV, I know you like that. You can go back to being Doris whenever you want, but you must have a rest first.'

Bo hadn't been prepared to admit it, but she was grateful for the break, and did all the things that the spaniel had suggested, and more.

One evening, she found herself alone in the house.

She didn't mind this. She enjoyed the freedom, as long as it wasn't for more than few hours at a time, and there were no thunderstorms. She would have liked to think she got up to huge amounts of mischief, but in reality she spent most of the time asleep.

The one thing she always investigated was the top of the table in the living room. It often had discarded chocolate wrappers, pencils or empty crisp packets, all of which were worth having. To reach these treasures, Bo had to climb onto the arm of the sofa and lean across the gap between it and the table. She could then swipe at anything of interest until it came within her reach or fell to the floor.

That night, there was nothing remotely chewable on the table, but what did catch Bo's eye was the front cover of a magazine. There was something very familiar about its craggy coastline and azure blue sea.

Bo stretched out a paw and nudged at the magazine until it was hanging over the edge of the table. Then she gave it a quick push and it hit the floor with a smack and fell open at its centre spread.

The right-hand page had a picture of high cliffs covered in small, gnarled trees, and a view over turquoise waters to a distant island.

Bo leant forward and examined the picture.

'So strange,' she muttered to herself. 'I feel as if I've been there.'

She scratched the underside of her chin with a hind foot.

'I need to ask Cavendish about this,' she said aloud.

She grabbed a corner of the magazine in her teeth and dragged it backwards in the direction of the door. It was an ungainly business, and she'd only managed a few strides when she reversed into something. She let go of the magazine and turned around.

At first she was unable to say anything.

She just stood there with her mouth open.

'Good evening,' said Cavendish courteously.

'What are you? I mean, how did you?' Bo stammered.

'Get here?' the spaniel offered. 'I'm not sure, but I've done it before. I've sat over there,' he said with a nod to the fireplace, 'and there, too,' he added, pointing to the window seat.

'You couldn't have. I'd have seen you.'

'You weren't here,' said Cavendish. 'No one was. It's taken me ages to work out how to do this. I've been practising for months, but only when the house was empty. I didn't want anyone to walk in, you see. I wasn't sure what they'd find.'

'Meaning?'

'Meaning I don't know how I'd appear to anyone other than you. You see me as a living dog. They might see nothing at all, or perhaps a hovering light. But what if I appeared as that badly stuffed old carcass of mine? What would they do then?'

'Scream, probably.'

Bo reached out and touched Cavendish on the nose.

'You seem solid enough to me,' she said.

'That's because you're you. If anyone else did that I'd probably crumble to dust.'

'Then they really *would* scream.'

Cavendish lowered a paw onto the magazine.

'What's this?' he asked.

'I don't know,' Bo replied, 'but it's very familiar. I was trying to take it to show you.'

'Let's have a look, then.'

They sat down together and Cavendish licked the underside of a paw so he could turn the magazine's pages.

'It's a travel brochure,' he said at last. 'The pictures are of Greece.'

'Is that why I recognise it? It looks beautiful.'

'Those gnarled trees are olives, and the ones with big leaves like hands are figs.'

'Doris hated figs,' said Bo.

She shuffled her front legs together and swallowed.

'Do you remember what happened in Greece?' Cavendish asked gently.

'Yes. Yes, I do. Isn't that odd? I've remembered something about Doris's life before I've even got there. I did that when I was being Mignonne in King Charles's time. I wanted to visit the children again. I had a feeling they'd played a very important game, and that Mignonne was there.'

'You were a time travel novice, then. It was your first ever flashback. These flashbacks are a part of your gift, Bo, but they won't always be about children's games. They can't always be good. Sometimes they'll show harder times. So tell me. Take a deep breath and tell me what you remember about Greece.'

'Well...' Bo began. 'The winter wasn't so bad. Antony and Cleopatra had a comfortable camp, our ships had shelter, and there was plenty of food and fuel. There was a good atmosphere, too. The soldiers were confident and Antony and Cleopatra were excited. They seemed more than strong enough to beat Octavian. Then, towards the end of winter, Cassius and Doris began to get that feeling I told you about. It was a just a feeling, there was no logic to it.'

'They felt something bad was about to happen?'

Bo paused.

'Yes,' she said. 'Antony had established ports all the way up the coast of Greece. He was in the best possible position, but then, at the first sign of spring, someone surprised him. They took the most important port right out from under Antony's nose. Then they sent ships to prowl the waters and search for the Egyptian grain carriers. They captured some, others turned back. Soon, Antony's men had nothing to eat.'

Bo looked down at the travel brochure.

'Those hills *look* green,' she said sadly, 'but there's not much to eat in them.'

'You can't feed a hundred-thousand soldiers on unripe olives and figs,' Cavendish agreed. 'And that sea *might* be teeming with fish, but you'd have to catch a million a week to keep an army properly fed.'

'Antony tried to get the grain ships through, but whilst his back was turned more ships crossed the seas. This time they landed in northern Greece.'

'What was in them?'

'Men. Octavian's men. Thousands of them. Antony was surrounded. He had enemy ships on one side and enemy soldiers on the other. He couldn't get away because he'd taken his own ships into the Ambracian Gulf for shelter. They were useless, anyway. They'd been sitting in the water all winter and were weighed down with barnacles and damp. It began to get hot. I mean *really* hot. The heat was searing. There was no cooling breeze, like in Alexandria, no green lawns, as in Rome. There was nothing. There *were* winds, but they only came in the afternoon and they were hot, too. The water in the gulf started to dry out. It wasn't long before the whole of one side of it was nothing but boggy marshland. Everyone said it was full of snakes.'

'And mosquitoes,' Cavendish added.

'Yes! *Trillions* of mosquitoes. Even when you couldn't see them you could hear them, especially at night. They made that horrible high-pitched whine of theirs. It was almost worse when they stopped, because you knew then that they'd landed on someone. Cassius and I got bitten all the time. We came up in little red bumps.'

'What about the soldiers and sailors? Did they come up in bumps?'

'Worse,' Bo muttered. 'Much worse. Antony used to take Doris to the infirmaries. He said it was nice for the soldiers and sailors to see her. They liked to stroke her.'

'Did Cassius go, too?'

'No. The men were shouting things, even though they were thin as rakes and covered in sweat. Antony said were delirious and that Cassius might frighten them.'

'They had malaria. It's carried by mosquitoes, though of course no one knew that then. If you're bitten by an infected mosquito, the malaria gets into your blood. When another mosquito bites you, she sucks up the infected blood and carries it with her...'

'Her?'

'Only female mosquitoes suck blood. She lands on her next victim, takes a bite, and infects him, too. And so it goes on. Malaria will spread like wildfire when people are packed close together. Antony was probably right about Cassius. Malaria makes people hallucinate, so a bedside visit from a lion might not have been the best thing.'

'Hundreds died,' said Bo. 'I don't think it was just malaria. There were other things, too. The men kept asking for water, but there wasn't any. Antony tried everything he could to make things better. He even challenged Octavian to a duel, but Octavian refused.'

Bo stopped talking.

'I don't remember much more,' she said.

'Do you want to go back again, Bo? You don't have to, you know. Not if it frightens you. We can leave things as they are. I can tell you what happened, if you'd like. Tell me what you want to do, Bo.'

'I want to see my friends,' Bo replied quietly. 'I want to see Doris's friends.'

CHAPTER THIRTY-EIGHT
Actium, Greece.
2nd September 31BC

Antony's generals and advisors had had different ideas about what he should do next, but all of them had agreed on two things.

First, Cleopatra must go home. Octavian had declared war on *her*, not Antony. If Cleopatra returned to Egypt, Octavian's soldiers might refuse to fight.

Second, Antony must avoid a clash with Octavian's sea admiral, Agrippa. This was the man who'd swooped on Antony's Greek ports and harried and captured the Egyptian grain carriers. Agrippa was known to be brilliant, his ships were in tip-top condition and he had well-trained, healthy crews.

Antony hadn't needed to hear about the dangers of Agrippa. He knew that a sea battle would be a disaster. Nor had he needed to be reminded about Cleopatra. He'd tried in the past to persuade her to go home, but the truth was he didn't really want her to. His generals were probably right about Octavian's soldiers, but what about the Egyptian sailors? Cleopatra wouldn't want to leave them behind, but even if she did so, it would probably be a waste of time. Her sailors were there for *her*. Where she went, they'd most likely follow, as might the eastern kings and their troops.

As for Antony's other options, some of his advisors had thought he should cut his losses, literally burn his boats, and then try to get his men overland to Egypt. Once there, they could eat and sleep in safety, build up their strength and return to fight Octavian on another day. Still other advisors had thought that if Antony could avoid Agrippa and act quickly enough, he might still beat Octavian on land.

Antony was a far better soldier than Octavian could ever be, but his army had been devastated by disease and hunger, and he had grave doubts about winning from such a bad position. He'd paced the floor of his tent for days and finally reached a decision. He would avoid any sort of battle. He would send his army to safety and avoid a clash with Agrippa, but he would also try to save his ships, and also those of Egypt.

Doris yawned and looked sleepily about.

Overnight, her room had been cleared of all of its contents. Nothing remained but her blanket, the couch she was lying on, and a silver travelling trunk.

'What's happened? Where's everything gone? Where's my...'

She shook her head and her eyes popped wide open.

She sat up sharply, heard her favourite collar jangle

against her fur and made a short grunt of relief.

'Hmph!'

The collar had been made by Antony from things he'd collected on the Greek beaches. He'd started with a beautiful pebble with a natural hole in it, then carefully selected special seashells, pieces of coral and water-smoothed fragments of broken pottery and glass. When he'd been happy with his choice, he'd strung the whole lot onto a knotted leather cord. The pebble was the centrepiece, and the result was Doris's most treasured possession.

'Good,' Doris muttered as she patted the collar with the back of her paw. 'At least they haven't taken *you*. I couldn't bear that.'

She jumped from the couch and trotted next door to Cleopatra's room. That had been cleared, too. All the queen's clothes, furniture and jewellery had disappeared.

Doris stood in the doorway and stared at the blank walls and deserted floor, then turned away and charged through the house. She inspected every room, and all of them were empty.

'We've been burgled,' she barked. 'We've been burgled and everyone's been kidnapped except for me!'

'Doris? Where are you Doris?' she heard Menander call.

She followed the sound of his voice and found herself back in her own room, where Menander was kneeling beside the silver trunk.

'There you are, sweetie,' he said. 'We're leaving.

Charmion and I have been packing all night. Your mistress's flagship is waiting in the bay with the rest of the fleet. Charmion's already gone out to her. All of your lovely things are safe. Look.'

Doris peered over the top of the trunk and wagged her tail approvingly.

'Do you see?' Menander asked. 'Here are your rugs, headdresses and collars. You have your favourite around your neck, so everything is safe. Now, let's go down to the sea,' he added as he lowered the lid of the trunk and locked it with a silver key. 'I think Cassius is already there.'

Cassius was sitting on the sand, looking across the bay. A rowing boat was making its way ashore, but the lion's attention was fixed on something else. He was riled. The tip of his tail was twitching, and his ears were flat against his head.

'He does not like the sea, you know,' said Menander. 'It makes him uneasy.'

'Rubbish,' thought Doris. 'He's been travelling all his life. He's very accustomed to the sea. There's something else out there, and it's making him very angry.'

As a precaution, she barked to let Cassius know she was coming, then trotted up behind him.

'What's up?' she asked nervously. 'What do you see, Cassius?'

'Over there,' the lion replied. 'Way over there. Standing on that spit of sand.'

Doris peered across the bay, to where a ribbon of

beach glittered in the morning sun. She could just make out the silhouette of a lone horseman.

'I can't see that far,' said Doris. 'I don't have long-distance sight like you do. I can't see who it is.'

'Then I'll describe him to you,' Cassius snarled. 'He is wearing gold anklets and bangles.'

'A rich man, then?'

The lion tipped his head.

'Flash,' he added through clenched teeth.

'Go on.' Doris urged.

'He has a flag in his right hand. A signal, I believe.'

'*And?*'

'And he has no left arm.'

'Not Polygnotus!' Doris gasped.

'The very same,' Cassius replied.

'What's *he* doing here?'

'I've no idea, but it won't be good.'

The rowing boat had reached the beach by now. Doris's couch and silver trunk were being loaded onto it, and Menander had gone to fetch Cleopatra.

'I think the queen should know that Polygnotus is here,' said Cassius. 'We should try to get her to notice him, and we need do it *before* she gets into the rowing boat. Once we're on the other side of that,' he nodded to large rock which protruded from the water, 'we'll lose sight of the spit of sand.'

'Good thinking. What do you want me to do?' Doris asked.

'Go and meet your ma. Tug at her skirts, grab her wrist,

do anything you can to get her attention. Meanwhile, I'll stand up, look straight towards Polygnotus and roar my head off. Here she comes...quick, Doris, run up the beach!'

Doris raced towards her mistress and did exactly what Cassius had instructed, and more. She tugged at the queen's skirts, swung from her shawl, nipped at her ankles and mouthed her hands and arms.

'I *know*, Doris,' the queen laughed. 'It's *very* exciting! Antony is going to save our ships and take us home! Hush, now. You're tearing my clothes.'

'This isn't a game, ma,' Doris barked. 'I'm trying to tell you something.'

'Stop it!' Cleopatra scolded. 'Stop it at once! Menander? Pick her up, please, she's...'

Doris had never heard Cassius roar, at least not properly.

The penetrating, blood-curdling sound seemed to make everything stop dead. Except for the oarsman and the servants who'd been loading the rowing boat. They all screamed and threw themselves face down on the ground.

'What's got into Cassius?' Cleopatra wondered aloud. 'What is it? What's wrong?'

She knelt down and took hold of Doris's front paws.

'Doris? Are you and Cassius trying to say something?'

'Yes! Watch Cassius! See where he's looking? That's Polygnotus!'

Doris turned towards the spit of sand.

It was deserted.

'Where's he gone?' she barked at Cassius.

'He's galloped off,' the lion groaned. 'He must have heard me. I did the wrong thing, Doris.'

'You did your best. That's never wrong. I don't think Cleopatra would have seen him anyway. The sun's very bright, she didn't know what she was looking for, and he was a long way away. We tried, Cassius, that's the main thing. And who knows? Maybe he wasn't up to anything at all.'

'You're very kind, Doris,' said Cassius glumly. 'But standing as far out to sea as you can get and waving a flag isn't normal behaviour. Polygnotus was up to *something*. We both know that.'

Cleopatra boarded the rowing boat with Menander, Doris and Cassius, and they were taken out to Cleopatra's flagship, the Antonias. Once there, Cassius and Doris made straight for the prow. Antony's ships were lying ahead of them in the shimmering Ambracian Gulf.

'I hope this works,' Cassius sighed.

'So do I,' said Doris. 'How many are there, do you think?

'About two-hundred.'

'Plus the secret. Don't forget the secret.'

Roman fighting ships weren't much more than immensely strong troop carriers. They used sails to get from A to B, but then fought without them, in shallow water. They did this by deliberately ramming each other until both sides were locked together. Then the slingers and archers would fire stones and flaming arrows whilst their legionaries leapt onto the enemy vessels. Only then was the real fighting done, on deck and with daggers and swords. For that, the decks had to be kept clear of clutter such as sails and rigging. No Roman fleet ever set out for battle with its sails on board. It was unheard of.

On that day, though, every one of Antony's ships was secretly carrying her sailing gear.

Antony's ships began to row towards the narrow channel which led out of the gulf and into the Mediterranean Sea. The Antonias and the Egyptian fleet followed at a distance.

'Can you feel it yet?' Doris asked.

'No,' Cassius replied.

'Come *on*!' Doris urged. 'Come *on*!'

She raised her head and searched desperately for the touch of wind in her face. It picked up every afternoon at about this time, and was always sudden, hot and brisk. Antony's plan was dependent on it. When the wind arrived, his ships would hoist their sails and drive into open water. Agrippa would be taken by surprise and, with no sails of their own, his ships would be left standing whilst Antony's made their escape.

'Come on, wind,' Doris said again. 'Where are you? Pick up! Pick up!'

'We have a problem,' Cassius growled.

'No, we don't,' said Doris, her nose still pointing in the air. 'It'll come. It always does.'

'No, I mean *another* problem. Look.'

Doris lowered her head, stared across the water and yelped.

A line of ships had appeared on the far side of Antony's fleet.

'Is that Agrippa?' Doris asked shakily.

'Yes.'

'Was he supposed to do that?'

'No. He has no reason to be out there. Unless...'

'Oh, *no*!'

'*That's* what Polygnotus was doing,' said Cassius. 'I *knew* he was signalling something. He must have found out about Antony's sails.'

'But *how? How* did he find out?'

'Snooping as usual,' Cassius surmised. 'He must have seen them being loaded.'

'And now our escape is blocked. We'll never get past that lot. There's hundreds of them.'

'Four-hundred, I'd say. Antony has half that many. He'll have to go on, though. He can't turn back now. If he does, Agrippa will chase him into the gulf and corner us all. We'll be annihilated.'

'Not me,' said Doris.

She lay on her stomach, wriggled towards the ship's rails and put her nose over the side.

'What are you doing?' Cassius asked.

'Preparing to jump,' Doris replied.

'Don't be ridiculous,' Cassius scoffed. 'You'll break into pieces. Or drown. Still, it'll be quick. That's something, I suppose. Better be quick than let *them* get you.'

'*Them*?'

'Shark, barracuda, moray eel. Take your choice. They're all down there.'

Doris backed away from the rails.

'Then I'll wait a little,' she said. 'See what happens.'

'Good idea,' Cassius agreed.

For a while there was stand off.

Both sides stayed where they were and glared at each other, but no one moved.

Cassius licked the underside of one of his paws and held it up.

'What do you see?' Doris asked.

'Not see,' Cassius said. 'Feel. I feel the wind. The wind is coming.'

The officers and deck hands on the Antonias had felt it too, and there was a sudden rush of activity as the Egyptian fleet scrambled to raise its sails.

'Hold on tight!' Cassius shouted as the hot wind ruffled his mane and lifted Doris's ears. 'I think we're going to make a run for it.'

Doris quickly grabbed Cassius's tail in her teeth and, sure enough, the Antonias's sails filled to bursting and she heaved to port.

Meanwhile, Antony's oarsmen had rowed closer to Agrippa's ships and the two sides had slammed together. Now their wooden hulls were grinding and crunching against one another, and making a terrific noise as oars snapped and splintered, and flaming arrows rained down and bounced off the decks. Fires had broken out, and there were screams and shouts as daggers and swords clashed and men fell overboard.

The Antonias headed straight for a gap in the mayhem. She swept through the smoke, the debris and the drowning men, and picked up speed. She ran out to the open sea with her fleet close behind her and didn't stop until every last one of them was safely out of danger. The Egyptian fleet, its queen and its treasure had made their escape.

Much later, a small, fast boat caught up with them.

On board it was Antony.

A rope was thrown to him and he climbed the steep sides of the Antonias's hull, but he didn't ask to see Cleopatra. Instead, he called Doris and Cassius to his side and walked with them to the stern of the ship.

'I thought Agrippa would attack from behind,' he argued as he sat down heavily on deck. 'That would be the normal way of things, and by far the best tactic for him. My plan was based on that very assumption. And it was a *good* plan. Had Agrippa chased us into open water as we expected, why then we'd have run up our sails and caught the wind! We'd have got clean away! Yet he drew ahead of us. Now why would he do that? There was no advantage in it. Not unless he knew we had our sails aboard.'

Doris glanced at Cassius.

'Which he did,' she sighed.

'As it is,' Antony continued miserably, 'Agrippa has captured or sunk two-thirds of my fleet. Yet *some* have escaped. That's the important thing. Fifty of my ships have been saved, and we can easily build more. The Egyptian fleet and its treasure are safe. My army is safe. Oh *yes!*' he exclaimed, punching the air. 'I still have my army!'

'Oh *no!*' Doris groaned. 'You don't think Polygnotus found out about that too, do you?'

CHAPTER THIRTY-NINE
Bo's House.
The 21st Century

'Well, somebody did,' Cavendish confirmed. 'Antony had sent his army overland to Egypt but Octavian managed to hunt it down. He bribed the soldiers to change sides.'

'No,' Bo shook her head defiantly. 'They wouldn't do that. Those were *Antony's* soldiers. They *loved* Antony.'

'They had no choice,' Cavendish replied. 'They were starving, diseased and exhausted and Octavian had blocked their escape route. Over the following months, he edged closer and closer to Egypt. Antony and Cleopatra tried to negotiate with him. They sent him money, they promised to retire to the countryside if he left them alone. Antony even offered to kill himself. But Octavian was relentless. He took their money but he didn't respond to their offers. News came that he was approaching Alexandria.'

'Antony and Cleopatra were trapped?'

'Yes, but even then, they didn't give in.'

'They were fighters.'

'They were always at their best when things seemed hopeless.'

'What did they do?'

'Just what you'd expect, really. They acted in character. Antony prepared to battle it out, Cleopatra stayed calm and practical. She made plans for every possible scenario but she was determined that, whatever happened, Octavian was not going to get his hands on Egypt's treasure.'

CHAPTER FORTY
The Royal Palace, Alexandria, Egypt.
August 30BC

Doris was very familiar with the tall, narrow building in the palace grounds, but she'd never been inside it. It had never occurred to her that such a structure might contain rooms and furniture. Now, though, she *was* inside it, and she could see that it was laid out like a little house.

The first room she came to had the usual arrangement of golden couches and side tables. She weaved her way past these, wandered to a doorway and stopped.

'How very odd.'

The entire next-door room had been filled with a giant heap of wood. It spread across the floor and reached to the ceiling. Doris could tell that it hadn't just been thrown together. This wasn't some random pile of timber. It had been carefully built. Linen tapers and bunches of dried grass had been stuffed into its crevices and it had an overwhelming smell of tar.

She found a small hole in the base of the heap and lay down beside it. She pushed her nose into the hole and sniffed. The tar was mingling with the scent of other things now, things like fabrics, spices and precious oils.

She wriggled further forward and saw skewers of sunlight. They were coming through chinks in the wood, hitting something and bouncing away. Doris realised then that the pile had been built as a hollow but then jam-packed full of something or other. She dragged herself into it.

'What the...?' she gasped.

There was barely enough space to stand.

She was surrounded by priceless gems, giant silver urns and ancient statues of lapis and gold. There were sackfuls of rare imported spices, bolts of gossamer linen and rolls of embroidered silk; necklaces of garnet and turquoise, ornaments of jade and jet, and ivory beads the size of cherries. Golden plates, jugs, bowls and dishes were stacked in tidy piles, and the gaps between them were filled with rivers of diamonds, emeralds, amethysts, pearls and sapphires.

Doris shuffled round and spotted a woven rush basket. It was lying on top of a whole sack of excruciatingly expensive Indian Ocean pearls. The basket had been carefully lined with a soft, camel hair blanket and then packed with Doris's favourite toys and collars.

She reached out and ran a paw over her purple collar of Isis. She'd been wearing it when Caesar was assassinated, but not since. The silk had faded and one of the lapis Iwiw charms had chipped, but the bloodstains were still there. Next to the Isis collar was the silver, diamond and river pearl 'sea foam' which she'd worn to sail to Tarsus and her first ever meeting with Antony. And here was the Dionysus headdress that Menander

253

had made. He'd been right. Dipping it in wax had indeed preserved it. After all these years, it was still recognisable as clusters of grapes on a circlet of lustred vine leaves. Doris sighed. Every one of these collars was special. Every one evoked fond or terrible memories. Yet now she pushed them gently aside and dug deeper into the basket to raise the most special of them all. Antony's shell necklace. She picked it up in her teeth. The scent of Antony's fingers still lingered on the knotted leather. She could feel the gritty sand of the Ambracian Gulf on her tongue and taste the cool saltiness of the collar's centrepiece, the pebble with its natural hole.

She heard footsteps and started.

The footsteps stopped beside the bonfire, and Doris was suddenly terrified. She remembered the flammable tar and the tapers of linen and grass. Was someone about to set light to them? Would they really torch all this fabulous treasure? What was it doing here, anyway?

She whimpered.

'Doris?' whispered a familiar voice. 'Where are you, sweetie?'

'In here!' Doris barked.

She struggled out of the bonfire and Menander knelt down so she could climb gratefully onto his lap.

'You've found your favourite collar!' he laughed. 'Did you like the little basket? I made it specially.'

He took the collar from Doris's mouth, placed it around her neck and tied its ends.

'There,' he said. 'Antony is on his way. He'll be so happy to see you.'

Doris waggled her tail.

'We must go quickly,' Menander added. 'We need to get to the very top of the building.'

They climbed flight after flight of marble steps. At the end of each one, Doris paused on a landing and peered into the surrounding rooms. All of them were stuffed with bonfires. Finally, on the uppermost floor, they came to a room which had no bonfire but Cleopatra and Charmion instead.

They were tying ropes to the furniture legs.

'*Now* what?' Doris wondered.

'You're just in time!' Cleopatra cried. 'Quick, Menander, put Doris down and take these.'

Doris watched, baffled, as Menander took the ropes' ends, hurried across the room and threw them out of the window.

Something banged against the outside wall.

'Good!' Menander exclaimed.

He turned to Cleopatra.

'They have propped a ladder!' he added excitedly.

There was a pause, and then a commotion on the ground far below. Suddenly, the ropes tightened with a thwack, the furniture they were tied to leapt and jumped, and Cleopatra and Charmion sat down to hold it still. They checked that their knots were holding fast, then they and Menander gripped the taut ropes and heaved and hauled. Their knuckles showed white and their faces turned red. The ropes sawed against the sharp stone of the window ledge, their tidy plaits furred, and they began to unravel. Doris was certain they would snap but, just then, two wooden poles appeared above the level of the sill. Menander grasped these tightly, one in each hand, and shouted to Cleopatra and Charmion to keep pulling. The poles edged forward, and Doris realised they were the ends of a stretcher. She could see the top of a man's head, then, bit by bit, his neck and shoulders. When the stretcher was halfway into the room, Cleopatra and Charmion dropped the ropes and ran to help Menander lower it gently to the floor.

'Antony!' Doris barked. 'It's Antony! What's happened? What's wrong with him? Why's he lying down like that?'

She could smell the salty scents of seawater and sweat, but something else besides. She reached Antony and realised that the other smell was blood. It was seeping through his tunic and creeping across the floorboards.

'Antony's bleeding!' she yelped. 'Somebody do something! Antony's bleeding!'

She watched helplessly as Cleopatra sank to her knees and used her silk skirts to dab at a gaping wound in Antony's stomach.

Menander turned to Charmion.

'Get some linen,' he ordered. 'Downstairs. Quick!'

The queen's skirts were sodden by now, so she reached behind her head and fumbled with trembling fingers to undo the pins in her hair.

'Help me!' she pleaded. 'Help me!'

Menander stepped forward to remove the pins, and Cleopatra's hair tumbled loose. She pressed it against the wound and tried to stem the flow of blood until Charmion returned with a bolt of linen from one of the bonfires.

'Please, mistress,' Charmion begged. 'Let me do that.'

Cleopatra moved reluctantly aside, Charmion unravelled the linen, and she and Menander began to bind Antony's stomach.

'What can *I* do?' Cleopatra asked. 'I must do *something*. What shall I *do?*'

'Bring some wine, perhaps?' Charmion suggested.

'W-w-wine?' Cleopatra stammered. 'Oh, yes, of course.'

The queen struggled to her feet and stumbled across the room. Tears were streaming down her face and her hands were shaking as she poured the wine and returned to Antony.

She knelt down and held the cup to his lips.

He took a sip and Doris crept closer and put her head on his shoulder.

His face was grey with battle dust and exhaustion and his thick, dark curls were matted with sand. He leant sideways so that Menander could knot the ends of the linen. Then, with the bandaging complete, he laid one arm across his chest and used the other to raise himself up. Like this, leaning on one elbow, he explained how he'd spent the morning making a final, desperate attempt to stop Octavian's troops from entering Alexandria.

'I battled to the last,' he said, 'but it was no good.'

He raised his hand from his chest and locked fingers with Cleopatra.

'Alexandria has fallen,' he added. His eyes were brimming with tears. 'I'm so sorry.'

'It doesn't matter,' the queen whispered. 'It is not important now. We will think about it later, but first we must get you well again. We must treat this terrible wound. Who did this to you?'

'Me. It was me.'

'You must not blame yourself, my love. It is a battle wound.'

'No,' Antony insisted. 'It was me. When I knew the fight was lost, I headed back to my quarters. I wanted some time to myself. Time to clear my thoughts before I came to see you. It was then that they told me you were dead. They said you'd killed yourself.'

'Who? Who said that?'

Antony shook his head.

His body shuddered and he stopped talking.

He lay back and closed his eyes.

'What's he *doing?*' Doris whimpered. 'Wake him *up, ma!* Wake him *up!*'

Menander stroked her back.

'Give him a moment, Doris,' he said. 'Let him catch his breath.'

Antony's eyes opened again.

'It was a misunderstanding,' he said at last, 'but when I heard you were dead, I gave my sword to my manservant and asked him to kill me, too. He said he couldn't. He turned the sword upon himself instead. So I took another...'

'And then heard that I was still alive...' Cleopatra

groaned.

Antony nodded.

'I asked my servants to send word to you...'

'We received it.'

'...and then carry me here.'

'We were waiting for you.'

Cleopatra stroked Antony's hair away from his forehead and bent to kiss him.

'And now here you are,' she whispered. 'You're safe.'

'Talk to Octavian,' Antony pleaded. 'Try to keep *yourself* safe. Ask him to spare you and the children. He might yet listen.'

'We will talk to him together. We will go to him together. When you're better.'

'You must remember,' Antony said.

His breath was shallow and rasping.

'I will.'

'No. I mean you must remember the good times.'

He lifted his arms and tried to fold them around Cleopatra but he was too weak, so he stretched out a hand instead and gently touched her face.

'Don't be sad,' he said as Cleopatra's tears trickled over his fingers. 'I've had a wonderful life.'

'And there's more to come,' Cleopatra sobbed. 'Much, much more...'

'No. No more,' he sighed. 'Is Doris here?'

'Yes,' Cleopatra replied. 'She's right next to you. Can't you see her?'

'No. I can't see anything. My sight is gone.'

'Then give me your hand...There. There she is. This is Doris.'

Doris watched in silence as her master blindly explored her fur. She was voiceless now. She couldn't even whimper as his fingers settled on her seashell collar.

'Little Doris Of The Lovely Hair, my precious friend,' he said. 'Take care of your ma.'

His fingers closed around the pebble with its natural hole.

'Take care of your ma when I am gone...'

'*NO!*'

'Don't go,' Cleopatra begged. 'Please don't go. Antony? *Talk to me. Talk to me, Antony! ANTONY!*'

'Good bye, my darlings. Good bye.'

CHAPTER FORTY-ONE
A few days later

Cleopatra and Doris lay beside Antony's body until it turned cold. By then, their hiding place had been discovered by Octavian's soldiers. The soldiers stomped up the stairs and were met at the top by Doris, who growled and snarled as they took her dead master away.

Meanwhile, Octavian took over Cleopatra's palace and, since no one had remembered to set light to the bonfires, he took all the treasure of Egypt, too, and put the queen under guard.

For days, Cleopatra and Doris barely moved, but lay curled up together, pining for Antony. The queen was pale, her eyes and lips were puffy from crying, and she wouldn't eat. Doris wouldn't eat, either. Menander and Demetrius tried all manner of things to tempt her, but she was just too miserable. She was losing weight, her coat was dull, and she didn't care. All she wanted was Antony. She was still wearing the seashell collar. Menander tried to remove it, once. He said it needed a rinse, but when Doris snapped at him for the first time ever, he held up his hands and backed off.

At last, Doris ventured into the gardens to get away from things and breathe some fresh air. She also wanted to find Cassius, but most of all she needed to have a good howl. She knew this would upset her mistress, so she made her way to 'Windy Corner'. She thought the breeze would muffle her cries and send them out to sea, but she was wrong. Her high, plaintive voice could be heard all over Alexandria. When she finally stopped to draw breath, she heard a penetrating, blood-curdling noise. It was a sound she'd heard only once before, on the beach at Actium. On that occasion, it had terrified Doris and sent the servants and oarsmen diving for cover, but this time Doris thought it the best, most friendly sound she could possibly have wished to hear.

'Where are you?' Doris called back.

'In the dungeons,' Cassius replied. 'Octavian's soldiers put me here after Antony died. I could have fought them. I wish I had. But my strength had left me. I was too miserable to fight anyone. I feel better now, and so will you. I'm being good. I'm being very docile. I'm hoping they'll let me out soon. I'll tell you when they do.'

After that, Doris and Cassius called to each other two or three times a day. It was Cassius who pulled Doris out of her grief. She started to feel better, just as the lion had said she would, and then, one morning when she was at 'Windy Corner', she heard the news she'd been waiting for.

'I'm out!' Cassius roared. 'I'm in the gardens! I'm

under the mango tree!'

'Then I'm coming to find you,' Doris barked excitedly.

She was trotting happily towards the mango tree when she encountered an old enemy. She couldn't run. She wasn't as quick on her feet as she'd once been, and Polygnotus had her cornered. He grabbed her by the tail, hoisted her onto his hip, then pressed the stump of his missing arm into her fur and pinned her against him.

Doris yelped.

'Be quiet!' Polygnotus hissed.

But Doris wouldn't be quiet.

'Cassius! Menander!' she barked. 'Someone come quick! Polygnotus has got me!'

She barked for her life until, inevitably, the eunuch clamped his hand over her muzzle. His vice-like grip was even stronger than when she'd last felt it, on the night she'd got lost in Alexandria.

Doris had been silenced, but not before Menander and Cassius had heard her cries. Menander knew that these weren't playful challenges to a mongoose or a squirrel, nor were they a warning that strangers were about. They were desperate calls for help. News travelled fast in the palace compound, and everyone had heard that Polygnotus was back in Alexandria and working for Octavian. To Menander, Doris's bark could mean only one thing.

Cassius could see Polygnotus now. He was scurrying towards Octavian's apartments with Doris pressed against his side. The lion knew he could rescue Doris in an instant, if needs be, but only as a last resort. He decided to wait and see if Menander responded to her cries. Sure enough, Menander appeared, rushed across the lawns and waylaid Polygnotus outside the door to the apartments.

'What are you *doing*?' Menander spat. 'You're *frightening* her. How *dare* you?'

'I can do whatever I please,' Polygnotus sneered. 'And right now I'm taking this dog to Octavian. She will make a pretty pet for his daughter.'

'Never! Not this dog! I swear by the glory of Isis, that if Octavian so much as lays a finger on her, I will kill him with my own hands.'

'Don't be ridiculous,' Polygnotus retorted silkily. 'And watch your tongue. Octavian has had them cut out for less. Now stand aside or I'll call the guards.'

Menander stayed put.

He was trembling with fury.

'Give Doris to me,' he insisted.

Doris wriggled and was quickly punished by a jab in the eye from Polygnotus.

She squealed, and Menander stepped backwards and raised his hands in surrender.

'All right, all right,' he said.

He took one of Doris's paws and squeezed it gently.

'Do what he says for the moment, sweetie,' he told her. 'I'll wait here for you.'

'Waste your time if you like,' Polygnotus flounced, 'but she's not coming back.'

Doris had never met Octavian, but she'd heard a great deal about him over the years. She knew he was scheming and clever. She'd also been told that he didn't like fighting and used to run away at the merest hint of battle. So when the doors to his apartments swung open, she expected to see a slight, rather sickly creature. Someone not unlike Cleopatra's tiresome brother, Ptolemy.

What she *actually* saw was someone who both outraged and surprised her.

She was outraged because Octavian was sitting on one of Cleopatra's thrones, and surprised because he wasn't at all as she'd imagined him to be.

He wasn't so much slight as compact. He had striking, fiery eyes, curly blond hair and bad teeth. He was very cool and calm. He didn't have the charisma of Caesar or the presence of Antony, but there was definitely an air of authority about him.

'So this is the dog,' he said imperiously.

He curled a finger and beckoned Polygnotus closer.

'It looks old,' he said as though referring to a piece of mouldy cheese. 'Will it survive the journey to Rome?'

'She is well-accustomed to travel,' Polygnotus replied.

Octavian stroked the side of his nose.

'It was a favourite of my great-uncle Caesar,' he said pensively. 'And is famous in Rome...I hear tell it was a close companion to Mark Antony. Does it eat a lot?'

'No, your greatness. She is very small and has an appetite to match.'

'It is of good temper?'

Doris growled and Polygnotus pinched her.

'Exceedingly so,' he replied.

Octavian sighed.

'I assume it is familiar with the lion?' he enquired.

'Yes,' replied Polygnotus. 'From the days of Caesar, and lately, Mark Antony.'

'Then it must also know Antony's mare. Does it?'

'Yes. She has ridden Ariadne many times. I believe they were together in Phraaspa and Armenia.'

'*Ariadne!*' Doris muttered. 'I'd *completely* forgotten about *Ariadne*! I wonder where she is?'

She made a mental note to ask Cassius about the horse, and Octavian continued with his interrogation.

'What does it have around its neck?' he asked. 'Something it scavenged from some god-forsaken beach, by the look of things.'

'It is a collar,' said Polygnotus. 'A collar made of shells. By Antony, I believe.'

Octavian sniggered.

'I always knew the man was a romantic fool...'

Doris snarled and received another pinch.

'She has more befitting collars...' Polygnotus interjected.

'*I* will decide what it *wears!*' Octavian screamed. 'Oh well...I'll take it!' he added without much enthusiasm.

Polygnotus stepped towards the throne.

'Not *now*!' Octavian snapped. 'I have no use for it *now*. Take it away! Let it stay with its mistress until the time comes.'

And he dismissed Polygnotus with a wave of his

hand.

When Polygnotus emerged from the apartments with Doris still in his arms, Menander burst into tears.

'Octavian will have her,' Polygnotus sneered as he handed Doris back. 'But only when he's ready.'

'Over my dead body,' Menander muttered as he carried Doris across the gardens. 'Now, Doris darling, we must return to your mistress, but first I have a surprise for you.'

At that very instant, Doris smelled the old, familiar scent of Cassius. She barked, and Menander laughed and let her run to where Cassius lay dozing in the shade of the mango tree.

'Hello Cassius!' Doris said as the lion got to his feet and padded towards her. 'It's so good to see you! I'm sorry I'm late. Did you hear me bark? Polygnotus caught me and took me to Octavian. He wants to take me back to Rome for his little girl, but I'd hate that, Cassius, I really would. I couldn't leave my ma.'

Cassius laid a paw on Doris's shoulder.

'You might not have to,' he told her. 'Octavian might take your ma and her children to Rome, too. He might march them through the streets in chains.'

'Cleopatra couldn't stand that. I think she'd rather die,' said Doris, 'but how do you know all this?'

'Because it's what Romans do. And because I've heard Octavian talking about it. He's adopted me, you know.'

'Oh, I almost forgot. I think he's adopted Ariadne as

well. Do you know where she is?'

'In the stables. He's been riding her. The poor creature's so docile and sweet, she just lets him. Why doesn't she buck him off? I would. He seems to think I'll cart him about in his chariot. Well he's got another think coming. The poor man's delusional. Can you imagine me doing that?'

'I don't need to,' said Doris. 'You did it for Caesar, remember? It was the first time we ever met. It seems like a lifetime ago now.'

Cassius nodded and lay down.

'It *was* a lifetime ago, Doris,' he said. 'And I am old and tired. We both are. My road no longer leads to Rome. I will not return there.'

'Not even if I went too?' Doris asked.

'No. Not least because Octavian has put Polygnotus in charge of me.'

'Ugh,' Doris groaned. 'Then I quite understand. What will you do, Cassius? Where will you go?'

'I will stay here, in Egypt,' Cassius replied. 'But not in Alexandria. I'll find somewhere else. Somewhere far away from people.'

'Won't you miss the company of humans?'

'Only those who are no longer with us. Caesar and Antony. Cleopatra. Whatever else she decides to do, she cannot stay here.'

'And me? Will you miss me?'

'Yes, Doris. I'll miss you *so* much that I'd like you to come with me. There will be nothing here for you soon, and you've said yourself that you don't want to go to

Rome.'

'There's still my mistress,' Doris replied. 'And Menander. He will never leave Cleopatra. I should stay with *them*, wherever they go.'

'You don't need to answer now,' said Cassius. 'Let's wait and see what happens. Oh, dear. Look what the cat's dragged in.'

Polygnotus was breathless and furious.

'This lion is the property of the great Octavian!' he screeched at Menander. 'It must not be visited, nor even set eyes upon, by the likes of you!'

He reached out his hand and patted Doris on the head.

'It's different for the dog,' he continued in a quieter voice. 'She, too will belong to Octavian soon. *She* may visit the lion. But not you, Menander. You're a nobody now. Your precious mistress is a nobody. Her lands and riches have fallen to my great master. They are possessions of Rome, now, just like this silly dog and that dopey mare of Antony's...'

Polygnotus ranted on. He was completely unaware of what was happening behind him. He couldn't see that Cassius was showing some rare but unmistakable signs of aggression. The lion's ears were flat against his head, his top lip was curled upward in a snarl, and the tip of his tail was twitching.

'It's only Polygnotus,' Doris pleaded. 'Don't let him get to you, Cassius. Ignore him.'

Cassius took no notice but transferred his weight

forward and lowered himself into a semi-crouch. He extended a foreleg. It hovered for a moment, then settled to earth with a sinister softness. In that one, simple movement, he'd travelled half his own body length.

He froze like that, and waited.

'*Please* don't do anything, Cassius. *Please*. He's not worth it.'

Polygnotus continued his diatribe. When he'd finished insulting Cleopatra, he had a go at Caesar.

'He deserved what he got. He had it coming...'

Cassius moved a hind leg, let it hover, placed it down.

'*Stop* it Cassius!'

In desperation, Doris turned her attention to Polygnotus. She yapped and tugged at his skirts in the hope of silencing him, but it was to no avail. The eunuch was on a roll.

Cassius crept closer.

'And as for that drunkard, Antony....'

Cassius sprang.

Doris saw his mane float out behind him, just as it had when he'd reached for Caesar's golden knife. She saw the toes on his dinner plate paws stretch wide. She saw his iron claws extend. She saw him swipe at the head of Polygnotus, heard a smothered cry and a horrible crunch, and watched the eunuch crumple to the ground.

Dead.

'The heavens and Isis!' Menander exclaimed as Cassius dragged the body into the undergrowth.

'*I* understand why you did that,' said Doris. 'But Octavian won't. He'll have you killed, Cassius. He won't want you as a pet now. He'll be too afraid of you.'

'Good.'

'You must hide. Please. Hide now, before they discover what you've done.'

'Not until you make your decision,' the lion replied.

'I've made it,' Doris fibbed. 'I'll go to Rome and be the pet of Octavian's daughter.'

'Rubbish,' Cassius snarled. 'I'll see you later.'

'Promise me you'll hide?' Doris begged.

'I promise. But first I'm going to free that soppy Ariadne.'

CHAPTER FORTY-TWO
A few days later

Doris raised her nose and listened to the cheerful tinkle of Antony's seashell collar. She sniffed, and smelled the blissful scents of Cleopatra's bath.

'One of Menander's special concoctions,' she concluded. 'Ass's milk, honey and myrrh. My ma's favourite. And here,' she added as she inspected the edge of the bath, 'are all of her favourite perfumes and balms, and a pile of warmed towels.'

She padded over to where Charmion was busy adjusting Cleopatra's costume of Isis. The handmaiden had spread the fabulous clothes across a couch. Here was the flower-embroidered gown, the star-spangled cloak and the golden headdress of cobras writhing through sheaves of corn. Here too, was the tell-tale mirrored disc which represented the moon.

The queen undressed and stepped into the bath, and Doris watched as Menander and Charmion sponged her ma's back with the fragrant milk, dried her body with the warm towels and smoothed her skin with the scented balms. Charmion then helped the queen into the costume of Isis whilst Menander plaited and pinned her hair and fixed the fabulous headdress. When the queen was ready, she moved to the salon next door and settled herself on a couch.

'Come up beside me,' she said to Doris. 'We are about to eat.'

Doris wagged her tail. The table next to the couch had been laid with a choice selection of Demetrius's repertoire. There was a platter of hippo liver, honey-roasted dormice and fresh oysters, several bowls of flamingo tongue and Black Sea caviar, plus jugs of wine and spiced beer.

Cleopatra piled plates for herself and Doris, poured herself some wine, then nodded to Menander and Charmion to help themselves. For the next hour or so, the queen chatted happily. She was back to her old self, giggling at Menander's jokes, reminiscing with Charmion, and passing tit-bits to Doris. Doris hadn't seen her mistress this happy for ages, and that made Doris happy, too. She didn't need to worry any more. Not about her ma, not about Octavian and the trip to Rome, not even about the trouble that Cassius had got himself into. Cleopatra was back on form, and no problem was insurmountable.

The meal was coming to an end and Charmion was clearing the table when there was a rat-a-tat-tat on the door. Cleopatra let out a little gasp and Doris sighed in disappointment. She thought Octavian's soldiers had come to break up the party, so she was surprised when Menander went calmly to the door and opened it.

The visitor was a man. He wore simple peasant clothes and was carrying a round, melon-shaped basket with a lid. He set this down on the newly cleared table, bowed to the queen and left.

Cleopatra glanced at the basket and pulled Doris closer.

'It is rumoured that Octavian will take us all to Rome,' the queen mused, 'and parade us through the streets in chains.'

'I don't believe that,' Menander retorted. 'It is too much of a risk, mistress. Octavian cannot possibly know who might be offended by it. Some could take it as a slur on Caesar, and there are still many supporters of Antony. I think Octavian has planted the rumour himself. To frighten us.'

'You may well be right,' the queen agreed. 'Antony asked me to talk to Octavian. Do you remember that? He said he thought Octavian might listen. That I might yet save myself and the children. I didn't do it. I couldn't see the point. Octavian ignored the offers we made at Actium, and afterwards. Why should it be any different now?'

'Good for you, ma,' Doris mumbled. 'You're right. Octavian won't listen. He'll *never* listen. He'll just spread the word that you came grovelling. He'll say the wicked eastern queen is on her knees at last. Hold your head up high, ma. Don't ever kneel for *him*.'

'Perhaps we should call his bluff,' Cleopatra giggled. 'We could say that our trunks are packed and we are ready to leave for Rome just as soon as he gives the word.

What do you think, Doris? You like Rome. Cassius and Ariadne are going too, by all accounts.'

'I'll do whatever you say, ma.'

'Or we could just run away. Menander could disguise me as a slave-girl and we could all run away. We'll find a little house somewhere. A mud hut, perhaps. We'll live on fresh fish by the banks of the Nile.'

Doris snuggled closer.

'That's sounds lovely,' she sighed. 'That sounds better than Rome.'

'The trouble with *that* idea,' Cleopatra continued as much to herself as anyone else, 'is that for as long as I am alive, Octavian will see me as a threat. He has taken my power, but he cannot take my powerful friends. He wouldn't rest, you know. Not until he found us. He would hunt us down. To be hunted is a terrible thing. The antelope out there on the plains? They cannot relax for a moment. They're always listening and watching for the predator that waits to spring. That is not the kind of life I want. It is no life.'

Cleopatra's musings and Doris's full tummy had almost sent Doris to sleep when her mistress reached out and removed the lid of the basket the man had brought. Doris had forgotten about the basket. Now she stretched her neck to see what was inside it.

'No, Doris,' Cleopatra said. 'They are figs. You hate figs.'

She pushed Doris away, then selected a fruit from the top of the pile.

'They are fun to play with, though,' she added as she

tossed the fig to the floor.

Doris watched the fig roll away but she was too soporific to follow it. She lay down again and rested her head on Cleopatra's thigh. She was more than ready for a nap, but then she noticed that Cleopatra was shaking. Something in the basket moved, and Doris sat up. The something moved again, and two or three figs fell onto the table. A head emerged from the basket. It had a blunt snout and peculiarly high-set eyes that were perfectly round. Its throat was pale and ridged, like the belly of a crocodile, and its forked tongue flickered like fire.

Doris shrank back.

'Don't touch that, ma,' she whimpered. 'Come away now.'

She turned towards Menander and Charmion.

'That's a cobra!' she barked. 'Throw something over it! What are you *doing*? Why are you just sitting there like that? Don't you have a cloth or something?'

She leapt from the couch and ran over to Menander. She wanted to force him into action but, just as she reached him, the figs on the table fell to the floor with a plop. She whipped towards the sound and saw the cobra rear. Its head flared and spread outwards like a hood and the scales along its back gleamed like polished stone. It weaved from side to side and hissed. It was a horrible sound. Deep and low and threatening.

'Get away now, ma,' Doris barked.

'Take hold of her, Menander,' the queen ordered.

'No!'

Doris yelped and wriggled, but Menander caught her

by the tail and scooped her up.

'So,' Cleopatra said calmly as she held an arm to the cobra. 'There it is.'

She poked the basket and the cobra's mouth shot open. It struck light lightning, wrapping its jaws clean around her arm and sinking its fangs into her flesh. She didn't scream. She barely flinched.

The snake hung on until its venom was spent, then it raised its head, had a quick look around the room, and sank quietly back into the warm darkness of the figs.

Cleopatra lay against her cushions with a sigh.

'Thank you, my friend,' she said.

As Doris ran to her mistress, Menander did exactly what she'd been urging him to do five minutes earlier. He threw a cloth over the basket, replaced its lid and removed the cobra from the room. Doris snarled at him and jumped onto her mistress's lap.

'You mustn't blame him, Doris,' said the queen. 'He has only done what I asked. Isis wears a crown of cobras, as have all the kings of my dynasty, and all the Pharaohs before them. It is a queenly end for me, but it will also be swift. I don't have much time now, Doris.'

Doris whimpered and shuffled deeper into Cleopatra's arms.

'Menander will take care of you,' the queen continued. 'He will make sure you are happy, whatever you decide.'

She stroked Doris's ears.

'Thank you, Doris,' she said sleepily. 'Thank you

for being my friend. Forgive me for the things I put you through. Caesar's murder, that dreadful time you spent with Antony in Media. I only ever wanted the best for you. And your masters. When I couldn't be with them myself, I lent them my Doris Of The Lovely Hair. I know you don't mind. I know you loved them too. I did ask Octavian one thing. I asked him to bury me next to Antony. Surely he cannot deny me that? We'll see. Come closer now, and be with me these last few moments.'

Doris snuggled against Cleopatra's neck and the queen bent to kiss her.

'Is it time, mistress?' Menander asked.

'Yes, Menander,' the queen replied. 'It is time.'

Menander delved into his sleeve and withdrew two phials and a small, muslin-wrapped packet. He nodded to Charmion, who was kneeling on the floor beside Cleopatra. The handmaiden was sobbing but she smiled, momentarily, and let go of her mistress's hand to take one of the phials. Then she broke the phial's seal and drank its contents.

Doris lay still as a mouse and listened for Cleopatra's every breath. Each was a little later and more shallow than the last, until the last was the *very* last, and Doris's ma was dead.

Doris buried her nose in her ma's warm hair and howled.

She sat up and howled some more.

She howled until she thought her heart would break.

The howls rang out across the palace gardens, over

the wall at 'Windy Corner' and far out to sea.

In the streets of Alexandria, people stopped in their tracks, and cats and dogs gasped and flopped to the ground.

And then came another sound. It was deep and primeval, a thunderous roar that resounded through the city and seemed to shake its very foundations.

Doris stopped howling, tipped her head and listened.

She ran to the window and looked out to where Cassius was standing in the palace gardens.

'You'll come with me, won't you?' the lion called softly. 'Only Menander is left, now. He could come too, if you like.'

'He will never leave my mistress,' Doris barked as Menander picked her up.

'And you?' Cassius asked. 'Will you leave your mistress?'

Doris pressed her head against Menander's shoulder.

'Would you like me to take you to Cassius?' he asked. 'Come on, then. Let's go.'

He carried Doris across the room. Beside the dead bodies of Charmion and the queen was the little table where the cobra's basket had sat. On top of it was the remaining phial and the muslin package.

'I must follow your mistress, as Charmion has done,' Menander explained. 'That second phial contains more of the poison that killed her. The muslin packet contains a roasted dormouse. Demetrius made it for you. It was the queen's last order, and his, too. He left the palace last night. You won't see him again, Doris. He's gone back to his village on the Nile. The dormouse is laced with poison. You don't have to take it, if you don't want to. You are an old lady now, but you can have a good life with Cassius. He will look after you. I am going to take you to him now, then I shall return here and watch from the window until you've made your decision. You understand that, don't you Doris?'

'Yes,' Doris replied. 'I understand.'

Menander kissed her and held her tight until she felt his hot tears trickle through her fur. Then he took her outside to Cassius and set her gently down.

'I will wait by the window,' he said again as he knelt beside her. 'If you return to the palace, I will feed you the dormouse and wait with you until it takes its effect. Only then will I drink the contents of the phial. Or you can stay with Cassius. Either way, you will never be alone.'

He laid his fingers gently on Cassius's mane.

'Take care of her,' he whispered.

He took Antony's shell collar in his hands.

'And as for you,' he added as he bent to kiss Doris on the head. 'Promise me you'll never remove this...'

'Not even to give it a rinse?' Doris whimpered.

'...not even to give it a rinse. And behave yourself. Don't go giving Cassius any trouble now, will you?'

Then he stood up and, without looking back, ran towards the palace.

CHAPTER FORTY-THREE
Bo's House.
The 21st Century

At the instant Menander reached Cleopatra's apartments, Cavendish returned Bo to her own time.

'I thought you might like a breather,' the spaniel said kindly. 'You can go back again, if you'd like. You can see for yourself what Doris did next.'

'No,' Bo replied. 'I don't think so. I don't think I can bear it. She must have been so torn. Anyway, I'm sure *you* know what she did. Do you? Do you know what happened?'

'Yes.'

'I thought as much. *How*? *How* do you know what happened?'

Cavendish lay down and put his head on his paws.

'You're always asking me what I know and how I know it,' he said. 'Quite right, too. Only the most inquisitive and questioning of animals are worthy of time travel. But even those who have the gift must also have a mentor. I am your mentor, and as such I will always know more than you.'

Bo looked sideways at the spaniel.

'Come off it, Cavendish,' she giggled. 'Don't give me all that "I'm your mentor, blah blah blah" stuff. Tell me how you know about Doris!'

'I know because I was there. I was there from the day the lions pulled Caesar along the Canopic. I was there until the very end.'

'Then...it was you. It was you all along. You were...'

'Cassius? Yes.'

'How? How were you Cassius? He was a cat. You're a spaniel.'

'Yes. And you're a poodle. But you were also a bird, once. Don't you remember that?'

'Of course I do. It was in the days of King Charles. I went back as Mignonne the poodle but I also became Sioluc the raven.'

'Exactly. So if you can be a bird, why can't I become a cat?'

'You can, obviously. But *why*? *Why* did you become Cassius?'

'So I could watch over you, silly. You don't really think I'd send you hurtling back two-thousand years on your own, do you? As soon as you told me your name was Doris I began my quest to find an animal that had shared her life. That animal was Cassius.'

Bo took a deep breath.

'I see,' she said again. 'Thank you, Cavendish. Thank you for watching over me.'

'My pleasure,' the spaniel replied. 'And now I can tell you what happened next, if you'd like.'

'Yes. Yes, please do.'

'Doris waited until Menander appeared at the window. She looked towards him, then at Cassius. She stood on her hind legs and wrapped her paws around the lion's neck. She was whimpering. Cassius thought she was going to leave him, but Menander knew better. He called good bye to her, and then he was gone...'

'He drank from the phial?'

'Yes. He killed himself. Doris was distraught, but she knew that she and Cassius had to hurry away. They left the palace for good and found a small village on the banks of the Nile. They were both very famous, of course. And sacred. But the villagers protected them. They kept quiet about their new neighbours, though they did tell one person...'

'Who? Who did they tell?'

'The queen's chef. Demetrius.'

'No!'

'Yes. He'd retired to his own village, just a little way upriver. Cassius and Doris were very well fed for the rest of their days.'

It was a long time before Bo spoke.

'Ariadne?' she finally asked.

'Ariadne escaped. Cassius slid the bolt on her door and chased her out of her stall. She galloped away and was found by a fisherman. He recognised her, fortunately, and had the sense to disguise her. He rubbed her all over with henna and charcoal, and she lived the remainder of her life as a happy but rather blotchy bay.'

'Menander asked Doris never to remove Antony's collar...' recalled Bo.

Cavendish raised a paw.

'Wait up,' he said. 'You haven't asked about Octavian.'

'That's because I'm not interested. I can't *stand* the man.'

'Octavian took the title Augustus Caesar and became the first Emperor of Rome. He lived to be very old.'

'Good for him,' said Bo. 'Now let's get back to Antony's collar.'

'Doris never removed it. She was buried in it.'

'Then it's safe, somewhere,' Bo mused. 'I'm glad of that. It was a very special thing. So simple. So beautiful. Do you remember it?'

Cavendish nodded.

'I remember it well,' he said. 'It had a pebble as its centrepiece.'

EPILOGUE

Bo caught Cavendish's eye.

'What?' she asked. 'Why are you looking at me like that?'

'Because I've been thinking about that pebble, and how much, much later, there was another one very like it. It was strung on a leather cord.'

'Just like Antony's collar?'

'Exactly like Antony's collar,' Cavendish replied.

'Who did it belong to?'

'A brave warrior, a brilliant horseman.'

'As brave and brilliant as Antony?'

'Maybe more so.'

'Wow!'

'Wow indeed.'

'Was he a cavalry commander? I like cavalry commanders.'

Cavendish chuckled.

'I know you do,' he said. 'That's partly why I chose him.'

'Chose him?'

'I thought you might like to go and visit him. See if he had a dog. Become his pet.'

'I'd need to know more about him, first,' said Bo. 'Was he *really* a cavalry commander?'

Cavendish shook his head.

'To be honest? No. At least I don't think he'd have thought of it like that. He saw the cavalry as the enemy. As his people's enemy.'

'But he rode into battle?'

'Certainly. He rode like the wind. He was one of the greatest horseback warriors who ever lived.'

'Was he like the Parthian archers?'

'*Very* like the Parthian archers.'

'Did he shoot arrows?'

'Yes.'

'*And?*'

'And the enemy he fought were the United States Cavalry.'

'The United States of America?'

'Yes.'

'*And*?'

'And he was a North American Indian, a Sioux Indian.'

'What was his name?'

'Crazy Horse. His name was Crazy Horse.'

The story of Bo's adventures as Dog Of Crazy Horse
will be told in her next book

IRON HORSES

www.bothepoodle.co.uk

PEOPLE AND PLACES IN MORTAL GODS

The dates and descriptions in this book are based on historical fact, as are the characters and locations. Here's what became of them all:

Alexandria was built by Alexander The Great. The original city is long-buried, but archaeologists are dredging the sea to find clues as to how it once looked.

Antony (Marcus Antonius) came from a noble but impoverished Roman family. He was an intelligent, charismatic and inspiring character whose soldiers loved him for his sense of humour and lack of airs and graces. Antony had a tendency to laziness and was a poor judge of character. He was married four times, though never to Cleopatra. Antony committed suicide in August 30BC.

Brutus (Marcus) was central to the plot to assassinate Julius Caesar, who'd always treated him like a son. Many people think he *was* his son. Brutus was chased down by Mark Antony and committed suicide in October 42 BC.

Caesar (Gaius Julius) had a brilliant mind and was a great statesman and military leader. He was assassinated on 15th March 44 BC. The Romans took over the island of Britain a hundred years after his death. They left in 410 AD.

Caesarion was Cleopatra's son by Julius Caesar. He was murdered on the orders of Octavian.

Canidius Crassus was a senior general in Antony's army. He admired Cleopatra and remained loyal to Antony. Canidius was executed on the orders of Octavian.

Charmion was Cleopatra's favourite handmaiden. She committed suicide with her mistress.

(The) Children of Antony and Cleopatra were twins, Cleopatra Selene and Alexander Helios, both born 40BC; and Ptolemy Philadelphus, born 36BC. All three were spared by Octavian. Cleopatra Selene married a King of Mauritania. It is not known what became of the boys.

Cilicia is now partly in Turkey, partly in Syria.

Cleopatra was a direct descendent of Ptolemy Soter, a general of Alexander the Great. The only corroborated portraits of Cleopatra are on coins forged towards the end of her life to illustrate her power and statesmanship. These show her as a hook-nosed dragon, whereas the real Cleopatra is known to have been extremely feminine, vibrant and witty. She had a deep love of perfume and cosmetics, an unusual knowledge of poison, and a gift for languages. She was the first of her three-hundred-year-old dynasty to speak Egyptian, and one of the few to master Latin. Cleopatra committed suicide in August 30 BC and was buried in Alexandria. Legend has it that Octavian granted her final wish and she was laid to rest beside Mark Antony.

Cobras are related to taipans and mambas. They vary in colour from black to yellowish white, and have muscles in their neck which flare into a 'hood' when they are threatened. The Egyptian Cobra, otherwise known as the asp, inhabits North Africa and the Middle East. It can live to be twenty-five and grow to three metres in length. It is extremely venomous and kills many people each year. Death is quick. It was almost certainly Cleopatra's chosen method of suicide.

Crocodiles have excellent hearing, sight and smell. The Nile Crocodile can grow to six metres. It lives in sub-Saharan Africa, the Nile Basin and Madagascar, and will attack anything within its reach. This includes about two-hundred people a year. Some victims are eaten immediately, others are stored in underwater larders.

Decimus (Brutus Albinus) was a close friend of Julius Caesar. He turned traitor and led Caesar to his death.

Egypt was conquered by Octavian and remained a Roman possession for over three-hundred years.

Ephesus is on Turkey's south-west coast and is one of the best preserved cities of the ancient world. Originally built by the Greeks, it was an important Roman port and trading post in Cleopatra's time and was later extended and modernised by Octavian.

(The) Gentleman who gave Caesar a scroll outside The Theatre of Pompey had once been the tutor of Brutus.

Hippopotami live in rivers and lakes in Africa. They cannot swim, but move around by pushing off from the riverbed or simply walking along it. Hippos are extremely territorial and aggressive. They kill more people in Africa than does any other animal.

The Kingdom of Commagene was in the most northern district of modern-day Syria.

Media is now partly in north-west Iran, partly in Azerbaijan.

Octavian (Gaius Octavius) adopted the title Augustus Caesar in 27 BC. He had a scheming, cold-hearted nature and a weak constitution, but he was also the first, longest lived, and arguably the greatest ever Emperor of Rome. He made sweeping changes to all aspects of Roman life and brought peace and prosperity. The month of August is named after him. Octavian mellowed with age and died in 14 AD.

DATES – all are BC

100		**Birth** of Caesar
83		**Birth** of Antony
70		**Birth** of Cleopatra
63		**Birth** of Octavian
61		**Birth** of Cleopatra's brother, Ptolemy
49		**Exile** of Cleopatra from Alexandria
48		**Exile** of Cleopatra from Egypt
	Oct.	**Arrival** of Caesar in Alexandria
	Oct.	**Return** of Cleopatra to Alexandria
	Nov.	**Outbreak** of Alexandrian Wars
	Dec.	**Burning** of the Egyptian fleet
47	Feb.	**Ambush** at the Heptastadion
	Mar.	**Victory** for Caesar and Cleopatra
		Death of Ptolemy, by drowning
	Spring	**Celebration** for Caesar and Cleopatra
		Cruise down the Nile
	June	**Departure** of Caesar from Egypt
	Sept.	**Arrival** of Caesar in Italy
		Birth of Caesarian
46	Oct.	**Arrival** of Cleopatra in Rome
44	Mar	**Assassination** of Caesar
		Return of Cleopatra to Egypt

42	Oct.	**Victory** for Antony over Caesar's assassins
		Suicide of Brutus
41		**Meeting** of Cleopatra and Antony at Tarsus
41	Winter	**Visit** by Antony to Alexandria
40	Feb.	**Invasion** of Rome's eastern territories by Parthia
		Departure of Antony from Alexandria to Asia Minor, then to Athens and Rome
	Autumn	**Marriage** of Antony to Octavian's sister
		Birth of Cleopatra's twins by Antony
39/38		**Withdrawal** of Parthia from Rome's eastern territories
38	June	**Withdrawal** of Parthia complete
37		**Agreement** between Antony and Octavian - ships for soldiers
	Autumn	**Reunion** of Antony and Cleopatra, in Antioch, Syria
36	May	**Invasion** of Parthia - Antony sets out from Zeugma
		Return of Cleopatra to Egypt to have her baby
	Oct.	**Loss** of Antony's artillery
		Retreat from Phraaspa
		Birth of Ptolemy Philadelphus, son of Antony and Cleopatra
	Winter	**Retreat** through Armenia

35	Spring	**Arrival** of Cleopatra, ships and food, in Luece Como, Syria
34	Summer	**Invasion** of Armenia by Antony
	Autumn	**Return** of Antony to Alexandria. He makes his children kings and a queen and makes Caesarion King of Kings
33/32		**Gathering** of troops by Antony, Cleopatra and eastern kings, in Ephesus
32		**Declaration** of war by Octavian on Cleopatra
32	Spring	**Movement** of Antony and Cleopatra and their troops, to Greece
31	Sept.	**Battle** of Actium
30	Aug.	**Conquest** of Egypt, by Octavian
30	Aug. 3	**Death** of Antony
30	Aug. 12	**Death** of Cleopatra and Charmion
27		**Elevation** of Octavian, to Caesar Augustus